LOVE FLUSHED

AN ALL ACCESS SERIES NOVEL

EVIE MITCHELL

THUNDER THIGHS PUBLISHING

Editor: Nicole Wilson, Evermore Editing
http://www.evermoreediting.wixsite.com/info
Proofreading: Ashley Lewis, Geeky Girl Author Services
Eileen Widjaja, Cover Illustrator

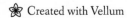 Created with Vellum

ACKNOWLEDGEMENT OF COUNTRY

I acknowledge the Traditional Custodians of the lands on which I write, the Ngunnawal people, and pay my respect to elders both past and present.

I acknowledge the continued and deep spiritual relationship of the Australian Aboriginal and Torres Strait Islander peoples' to this land, and their unique cultural relationships to the land, waters and seas, and their rich contribution to society.

BOOKS BY EVIE MITCHELL

Capricorn Cove Series

Thunder Thighs

Double the D

Muffin Top

The Mrs. Clause

Beach Party

New Year Knew You

The Shake-Up

Double Breasted

As You Wish

You Sleigh Me

Resolution Revolution

Meat Load

Trunk Junk

Dogg Pack Books

Puppy Love

The Frock Up

Pier Pressure

Bad English

Trick or Trent

Nameless Souls MC Series

CONNECT WITH EVIE MITCHELL

Facebook
Greedy Readers Book Club
Instagram
Amazon
Bookbub
Goodreads
Newsletter

To everyone who didn't panic buy toilet paper during the pandemic.
My ass thanks you.

And to my husband,
This book wouldn't have made it without you.

LOVE FLUSHED

It's about to go down...

Annie

I sell toilet paper for a living. It doesn't seem glamorous but S#!T HAPPENS is going places. We're the fastest growing eco-toilet paper subscription service around. We're amazing—and I should know, I'm my own best customer.

After years of hard work, I have everything I need to take my business to the next level—well, everything except the paper.

When my competition swoops in and offers my supplier a better deal, I'm left up a certain creek without a paddle. I must have done something truly crappy in a previous life because the only person willing to help is my ex-boyfriend, Lincoln 'Linc' Garrett.

The man is arrogant, infuriating, and far too attractive for his own good. Thankfully, I flushed any lingering feelings for him the moment he dumped me all those years ago.

So... how did I end up in his bed?

Linc

Annie and I were hot and heavy in high school. We were the golden couple, ready to ride off into the sunset for our life together.

Until my life went to poop and like the ass I am, I flushed everything good from it.

Now she's back in town and stirring up all kinds of feelings I thought I'd purged. Feels like desire, happiness, and something that feels a whole lot like—NOPE. It's not happening. No way. No how.

Or at least it wasn't. But when Annie's left with no choice but to accept my help, it seems as if my heart might have other ideas.

Looks like s#!t really does happen...

CONTENT WARNING AND TERMINOLOGY

This book contains references to addiction, cheating (not by the main characters), Crohn's disease, toxic and difficult parent relationship, and spanking.

The experience of Annie in this book is based on the Author's own experience of living with Crohn's Disease. Everyone's experience is different, and this book reflect mine.

While all care has been taken to ensure representation is respectful and inclusive, my sensitivity readers and my personal experience is limited to our own knowledge and understanding. If there is anything in the book that raises concerns for you, please feel free to reach out to EvieMitchellAuthor@gmail.com.

CHAPTER ONE

Lincoln

"How long do we have?"

"Best-case scenario?" Adam Bronze shrugged. "Maybe six months."

Shit.

I exchanged a look with my brother.

"And worst-case?" Theo asked.

"Three—if you're lucky."

Fuck, this hurt. I absorbed the blow with the same stoicism I'd displayed in every shitty conversation Theo and I had been subjected to over the last month, forcing myself to ask the hard questions.

"What do we need to do to get the mill back on track?"

Adam pinched the bridge of his nose. The guy didn't look like any accountant I'd ever met. Mid-thirties with a mop of sun-touched auburn hair and tan skin, he looked more like a surfer than a suit.

"I'm gonna level with you—a fuck of a lot. Your Dad's been borrowing hand over fist for years. Couple that with the lack of meaningful reinvestment, old machinery, and your narrow market...." He shrugged. "I just don't see how it's possible to recover."

The pulp and paper mill had been in our family for six generations. We employed two hundred people—failure wasn't an option.

"Humor us," Theo grunted, crossing his arms over his chest.

Adam blew out a sigh. "Well, for starters you'd need a cash injection to keep the lights on."

"How much?"

"At least two-fifty."

I nodded, mentally working out which assets we could sell off or remortgage to make the payment.

"And you'd need evidence of buyers—new contracts and nothing smaller than four years. You'd have to prove to a bank that you have long-term financial stability in order to get a loan."

"Another loan?" The new worry added a stone to the already heavy weight on my shoulders.

Adam nodded. "Lincoln, I know it seems like a lot but you need to update your equipment. The shit you have is costing you time and money. You need better perfor-mance, and you need to diversify."

"Diversify?". I'd been foreman for five years, and knew how obsolete the equipment had become.

"Copy paper and cardboard aren't going to cut it anymore. You need to move into other product markets—fast food wrappers, napkins, paper towels—

hell, even toilet paper. And renewables?" He dug through a pile of binders on his desk, pulling one free.

"This is a prospectus on the paper recycling market. I pulled it together for Walter last year." Adam paused, wiping dust from the binder face. "He, ah, he wasn't that interested."

"No doubt," Theo muttered.

"All you need to know is in here, but the main thing to consider is a move to recyclables. It's cost-effective, environmentally friendly—which is marketable as shit—and sustainable. Not to mention the profit margins are impressive."

Theo took the offered binder, flicking through the glossy pages. "What are we talking money-wise?"

"With more people choosing to use paper instead of plastic options, you're going to see immediate returns."

"A shift to recycling will mean outlays." I shook my head. "We can barely afford to pay our employees. How are we going to fund new equipment, training, research... those expenses alone would be prohibitive."

Adam reached across the desk to tap the binder. "It's all in here. The state offers grants for manufacturers looking to pivot. But a condition of the grant is your ability to prove you can support your workforce over the next five years." He glanced from me to Theo. "You need to find buyers. And not small ones—you need big contracts to land this."

Fuck.

"Right." Adam waved us off. "Go home, think about what I've suggested and let me know what you decide."

I rose, holding out a hand for him to shake. "Thanks. We really appreciate it."

He made a dismissive sound. "It's my job to help. And I'd hate if one of the town's oldest businesses—and biggest employers—died on my watch."

I swallowed the bile burning up my throat. "We're gonna do everything we can to make sure that doesn't happen."

Theo trailed me, an uneasy silence settling between us as we left the accounting office.

"Fuck," He slapped against the side of the building. "Our own flesh and blood. That fucking motherfucker."

I echoed his sentiment. "We need to speak to Walter."

"No, we need to report him. Call the cops. Get someone in to investigate what the fuck he's been up to."

I sucked in a breath, reigning in my rage. "We need to talk to him. He's the only one who knows the full story."

I jerked open the door to my old pickup, sliding into the driver's seat, and allowing myself the pleasure of slamming the door. Childish? Yes. Needed? Fuck yes.

"You really wanna see him right now?" Theo asked, tapping the binder against his leg. "We're more likely to strangle him than question."

"We've got no choice." I rolled my shoulders, trying to work out the tension. "Until we know the whole of it, we're gonna be working from a disadvantage."

"Gramps should never have left him the business."

I sighed "We both know our father is good at hiding his true colors. And Gramps—"

"Trusted him," Theo finished. "The old man only saw the good in people. Fuck."

In unison we scrubbed hands down our faces.

"How do you want to play this?"

I reached for the pack of antacids I'd begun carrying, popping one to chew.

Prior to a month ago my biggest concern had been what pizza to order. Then Walter had driven into a tree, and my whole fucking world had come tumbling down.

"No idea," I admitted. "I guess start with him and figure out the rest once we know."

Theo sighed, his eyes shadowed. "Do we tell the workers?"

"Fuck no." I shook my head. "Let's try and get out of this mess before we bring others into it."

I'd worked full time at the mill with my brother since graduating high school. My life had a routine and rhythm to it that, while not thrilling, had meaning. I couldn't imagine a future without the mill.

"Shit, I need a drink." I dropped my forehead against the steering wheel, anxiety churning in my gut.

"We could go to the nursing home and talk to Dad or we could hit a bar, get drunk, and deal with all this shit tomorrow." Theo tossed the binder onto the dash.

"Fuck it. Let's deal with the old guy tomorrow. Tonight, we drink."

"I'm down for that."

CHAPTER TWO

Annie

"Damn," I muttered, catching sight of the attractive men entering bar. "Damn, damn, damn."

Capricorn Cove was the kind of place where everyone knew or knew of everyone else. At one time I'd loved the community feel that smallness invoked, relishing that I knew all my neighbors by name.

Nearly a decade later, I couldn't think of anything worse.

"I spy with my little eye something beginning with ex-boyfriend," my cousin trilled from across the bar.

Looking at us, you wouldn't know Penny and I were related. I worshipped the sun, she lived for the moon. Thin and lean with porcelain skin speckled by a riot of freckles, Penny didn't look like the kind of woman who lived in a coastal town. She burnt if the sun so much as brushed her delicate skin.

"Shut your mouth." I gave the men my back, twisting

to fully face her. "Why are you bothering me? Shouldn't you be serving paying customers?"

She laughed, brushing a chunk of red hair away from her face, amusement flashing in her pale blue eyes. "Speaking of, where's your date?"

I glanced at my watch, my lips pursing into a thin line. "Late."

"Maybe he stood you up."

I sighed. "He wouldn't be the first."

She patted me on the hand. "If only you were into girls. All this could be avoided."

I tapped my chin. "You say that, and yet you're single. Something doesn't add up, cuz."

"The difference is that I *choose* to be single. While you?" She waved a hand toward her patrons. "Slim pickings."

Isn't that the truth?

"Anyway, I thought you were meant to be at that big trade show this weekend?" she asked, picking up a glass to polish.

"Next weekend." I glanced at my watch for the fourth time in as many minutes. "Friday to the following Tuesday."

"Got your pitch ready?"

I nodded, terrified as a big, warm, familiar body slid into the space beside me.

"Hey you two, what can I getcha?" My cousin switched to customer service mode, discarding the dish rag and half-polished wine flute.

"Two beers, whatever's good on tap. Thanks Pen."

I stiffened, leaning away from the man beside me.

Lincoln Garrett.

Big and broad, he'd seemed to be constantly adding muscle and bulk to his already large frame. The boyish awkwardness with which I'd once fallen in love had disappeared, leaving in its place the graceful stride of a man completely at one with his body.

Fine lines had begun to form at the corners of his mouth and eyes, memories of laughter beginning to carve grooves into his skin. A dark beard covered his blunt, square jaw, and rather than hide, it seemed to emphasize his sensual lips. His dark eyes could still pierce me from across a room, his gaze a familiar caress.

Resist, girl! Resist!

"Hey, Annie." Linc leaned against the bar, his massive forearms settling on the dark wood. "Good to see you."

I twisted, pasting a pleasant smile on my face. "Hello, Sir Shithead." I leaned forward a little, nodding at his brother. "And Theo. How are you?"

"Doing alright," Theo said with an amused grin. "You gonna give Sir Shithead here a hard time? 'Cause we've had a rough day."

I sized them up, noting the tension in their shoulders and the crinkles around their mouths and eyes.

I looked back to my drink. "You may sit beside me quietly. I'm waiting for someone."

They grunted in unison, both pulling out a stool to take a seat.

The twins were identical—or at least they had been, until Theo's accident. He'd lost his right leg and now used a prosthetic.

I shoved the memories away, determined to focus on my upcoming date.

"You look nice," Linc finally said after an prolonged silence.

"Thank you. I know."

"On a date?" Theo asked.

"She's meant to be but I think he stood her up." My traitorous cousin slid their beers across the bar. "You should all go play pool. Cheer each other up. You're ruining the vibe over here."

I shot her a look that promised retribution which she —predictably—ignored.

"You're dating?" Theo cocked an eyebrow.

I'd always been able to tell them apart, even as kids. Theo asked the questions, always wanting to know more. Linc made the decisions. A natural born leader, where he led others followed.

And for a long time, I'd been willing to let him lead me anywhere.

"Dating," I finally said, answering Theo. "Is a mild term for the hell of Capricorn Cove's singles pool."

He snorted, raising his beer. "I'll drink to that. If you're not related to them, you've already dated them."

"Or they've dated your friends."

"Or your family."

"Or they're divorced."

"Or there's a *definite* reason they're still single."

We grinned at each other .

"Maybe you two should date," Penny offered, watching us with a mischievous smile.

"What?"

"Fuck, no." Theo shuddered. "We'd kill each other within five minutes."

She placed the glass she'd been polishing back in its rack. "And yet here you are bantering back and forth like lovers. Perhaps there's something there?"

I wanted to reach across the bar and cover her mouth to prevent more stupidity from spilling out.

"There's not." Linc shoved to his feet, grabbing his beer. "A relationship needs sexual chemistry and these two are purely platonic."

I hated that he knew that.

I opened my mouth to protest only to be interrupted by my cell beeping. I glanced down, swiping to read the text.

Parker: Hey Annie, I'm going to cancel. I'm a bit wasted after drinks with the boys. Raincheck?

I stared at the message, irritation popping like corn kernels under heat.

Oh, you want a raincheck do you?

I tapped out a quick reply.

Annie: Raincheck? You cancelling a date when you're already thirty-minutes late is not only disrespectful, it's downright arrogant. Talk about a douchebag move. Goodbye Parker.

I sent the message then tossed my cell back in my clutch, muttering curses directed at the douchebag men of the world.

"He stood you up?"

I shot Linc a glare. "You really want to ask that question?"

He raised his hands in surrender. "Hey, I'm just

saying, his loss."

I slid from my stool to a stand. With the extra inch from my wedges, I could meet his gaze straight on.

"You'd know all about that, wouldn't you?"

I twirled, storming from the bar, determined to pledge my allegiance to the only men in my life who mattered—fictional characters.

Linc

I watched Annie retreat, her irritation drawn around her like a cloak.

Magnificent.

She paused in the doorway to the bar, her golden eyes flashing. She threw me one last glare before pushing through the doors and disappearing out into the night.

My body displayed a Pavlovian response to her annoyance, aching to bury my dick deep between her welcoming thighs.

In high school, we'd been inseparable. Hot and heavy, she'd been one the best parts of my life—still was, if I was honest. Annie had a flair for the dramatic, and had loved nothing more than to rile me up. I'd been conditioned to interpret her annoyance as desire—and fuck if I wasn't hard as a fucking post.

"She looks good," Theo commented mildly. "Curvier though."

And she wore every one of those extra pounds perfectly, her body a lush feast I wanted to explore.

I grunted, turning back to the bar, gulping my beer.

"That dress...." Theo whistled long and low. "Almost makes me wish I was attracted to her."

I bristled. "I know what you're doing. Stop it."

"So the image of her in that skintight green—"

I shoved him, ignoring his laughter. "You gonna chat all night or drink?"

Theo watched me with the same dark eyes I saw reflected every morning in the mirror, his expressions as familiar as my own.

He shrugged. "Let's shoot some pool."

"Winner doesn't have to speak to Dad tomorrow."

Theo shuddered. "Get ready to lose buddy."

He handed me one of the cues. "I never thought she'd come back."

I rubbed my thumb over the tip, feeling the chalk end. "I did."

"Really?"

"Mhmm." I reached for the powder cube, grinding it into the tip. "She cares too much. She couldn't leave her family behind."

"Isn't she some big shot entrepreneur now?"

Pride burned in my gut. "Yep. Toilet paper."

Theo perked up. "Really? Maybe we could—"

I cut him off. "Don't even say it. It's not happening. Even if I wanted to, she wouldn't go for it."

"Damn." Theo watched as I broke the racked balls. "Guess we're back to the drawing board."

"Yep."

"Story of our life."

We picked up our beers, taking a long pull.

"Absolutely sure you couldn't convince her?" Theo asked, resting his glass on the side of the table, lining up his first shot.

I didn't bother to answer.

CHAPTER THREE

Linc

Nursing homes freaked me out. Maybe it was the unique mix of piss and cleaning products that hung in the air, maybe it was being faced with my own inevitable mortality, or maybe they reminded me too much of pounds—where people and pets were dropped off and rarely returned home.

Either way, they were one of my least favorite places to visit.

I trod the familiar path to Dad's room, waving at the nurses and residents as I passed.

Walter Garrett had never been much of a father. He'd say he'd done the right thing by marrying my mother after he'd knocked her up, and for a brief time he'd even tried—committing to putting food on the table, and occasionally attending an obstetrician appointment.

But from the very beginning Walter had only cared about one person—himself. Little in this life held his interest for long, as our mother had discovered the hard way. With two kids under three, and a husband who spent more time in others beds than his own, she'd finally left him—and us—just three short years into their marriage.

I couldn't recall even one instance of my family sitting down for a meal together, such was the animosity between my parents.

"Fucking Theo," I muttered, hovering outside Dad's door. "Fuck. Let's get this over with."

I found Walter tucked into his bed watching a daytime soap on the small TV. From this angle he looked fine—a little salt and pepper in his hair, a few wrinkles marking his face—he looked like any other guy in his early sixties.

"Linc," he slurred, twisting to gesture with his good hand. "Come in."

And then there was the other side of his body. Now turned to me, I could see the effects of the crash in full light—the bandages across one side of his face, the lack of movement from his damaged arm. The blanket hid the worst of his injuries—a shattered leg, a busted hip, and two severed toes.

Used to seeing him upright and fighting fit, this change still cut me deep—made worse by the fact I had to deal with the fallout of his choices.

"Dad," I greeted, taking a seat beside his bed. "You're looking well."

"Better," the old man agreed. "Therapy helps." He glanced at the door behind me, his expression expectant. "Where's your brother?"

Fixing your fuck up.

"At work."

We fell into an uneasy silence, both of us watching the shitty TV program.

"Why are you here?" he asked when the episode ended, credits beginning to roll down the screen.

I sighed, unable to put it off for any longer. "I need you to sign over power of attorney to Theo and me. We need to make decisions about the business."

Dad waved his good hand dismissively. "I'll be out of here soon."

"No, you won't." I looked pointedly at his legs. "The doctor said—"

"He doesn't know what he's talking about."

"Oh, so you know more than a guy with twenty years of medical experience?"

Walter shot me a glare. "Watch your tongue. I might be laid up but I'm still your father. I can still whip your ass."

I pulled the papers from my back pocket, tossing them on the bed. "We spoke to Adam. Best-case scenario, the mill has six months. The family can forgive you a lot, Dad. The drinking, the fucking around, the spending. But to fuck with the mill?" I shook my head. "That affects this town. That affects this family." I pounded a fist to my chest. "That affects me.

He bristled, straightening in the bed, his face color high. "Now see here, Lincoln. I—"

"Fucked up." I crossed my arms over my chest. "You fucked up, Dad. And you keep doing it over and over again. You ran the business into the ground. You borrowed money to fund your drinking and gambling. I'll give you props—you managed to hide it pretty well. But now?" I tapped the papers on his lap. "Now you gotta do what's right."

"And that's letting *children* run my company?" he sneered.

"That's letting Theo and I do what we do best—fix your fuck ups." I gestured at the room. "Your recovery is contingent on the business not failing. It goes under and all this disappears."

His jaw clenched. "You ungrateful fucker."

I let him rage, his words easily washing off me. I'd spent too many years living around Walter to let myself absorb any of his bullshit.

"Here." He gathered the papers. "Give me a fucking pen. I'll sign 'em. Betrayed by my own fucking blood."

I stepped from the room, searching the large atrium for our solicitor.

"He's ready for you."

I'd hired Scott, and asked one of the nursing home doctors to certify Walter was of sound mind and health as he signed—grumbling and complaining—the papers. I couldn't afford any mistakes.

"And that's it," Scott said, checking them over one final time. "I'll file today but you're good to action anything you need."

"Thanks." I clapped a hand on his back. "Appreciate your time."

He chuckled, tucking the papers into an envelope. "Don't thank me. You're paying for it."

He and the doctor left, leaving me alone with Dad.

"You happy?" Walter seethed, glaring at me from the bed. "Satisfied?"

I stared at him, once again disgusted that I shared blood with a man like him.

"No," I said finally. "Not even fucking close."

With curses ringing in my ears, I left to do what I always did—clean up his mess.

CHAPTER FOUR

Annie

My LOVE LIFE might have been an epic fail, but—I had to admit—my business looked to be booming.

The sanitary trade show had started two days ago, featuring everything from the latest toilet improvements to production and supply chain changes. The poop had power.

I'd spent my time wisely, absorbing everything I could from keynote speakers, reps, and manufacturers. But today was my day to shine—today was pitch day.

"As you can see," I explained to the executives in the room, clicking through my presentation. "Shit Happens has seen a two-hundred percent growth in the five years since I founded the company. After operating expenses, reinvestment, and donations, we're on track to make a three million dollar profit this year."

I clicked to the final slide in my presentation, and nodded at the potential buyers. "Our numbers are solid, our market is growing, and we have an excellent reputation here and overseas. People want our product. They want toilet paper and sanitation products that are eco-friendly. I'm happy to take questions."

I'd founded S#!T Happens five years ago after running out of toilet paper mid-flare. Living with Crohn's disease sucked. Living alone with Crohn's disease was its own special kind of hell.

After running out of toilet paper—and then being delivered some one-ply bullshit—I'd lost my temper and decided to set up my own subscription-based sanitary company. S#!T Happens, my million dollar company, had literally been born on the back of a toilet roll.

"I like your figures," a bald guy from one of the big brands said, knitting his fingers together. "But rumor has it you're reliant on your current supplier for the products, and they're not coming to the party."

I pursed my lips. "My supplier and I are in negotiations to extend our existing arrangement. As I noted in the presentation, our focus is being sustainable. Our current supplier had a few areas where we felt they could be doing better."

The executives—mostly older, white men—nodded.

While S#!T Happens was currently subscription only, I wanted to move us into brick and mortar stores. This pitch to interested reps from big-name grocery and retail chains had the potential to help me realize that dream—if they decided to negotiate.

"I'm not sure about the name," a man said from the back of the table. "It's vulgar. Our store wouldn't be able to carry it."

I clicked back through the slides, finding our buyer information.

"Millennials and Gen Z are our primary target markets. These are people who are socially responsible, enjoy a pun, and want to give back to society. They're consciously-minded and care about minimizing their impact on the environment. And they influence their parents' buying habits."

I clicked to the next slide to show projected growth figures. "Our products speak directly to these buyers. The name is recognized and trusted."

The questions continued, coming hard and fast as I fought to defend my product.

"Well." The sole woman in the group stood, smoothing her skirt. "I'm sold."

She walked around the long conference table, hand outstretched. "Annie, it's been a pleasure. We'll send through the terms of our contract this week for negotiation."

My heart leapt into my throat, my body vibrating with excitement. "Thank you, Tara. I appreciate you coming today."

She clasped my hand and leaned in. Her perfume tickled my nose as she dropped her voice to whisper in my ear.

"You'll lose the three at the back—they're going with your competition. But throw Green and Webster a bone and they'll run you for two years as a trial."

I pulled back slightly. "Why are you telling me this?"

"I believe in you and your product." She gave my

hand one final squeeze, her brown eyes dancing. "And us women need to support each other."

She stepped back, dropping my hand to turn to the room.

"Gentlemen." Tara inclined her head, silver hair catching the light as she left.

"I'm out." The rep from Hollander Foods dropped my information kit back on the table. "Your competition has better prices."

"But less sales and they're not as eco-friendly. I've done my research, Carl. I know the market. There's no one doing what we're doing for the same price."

He snorted, shoving away from the table. "I'm still out."

"Thank you for coming."

He waved me off, leaving the pitch room, a few other reps following.

And then there were two.

I looked at the final two men in the room, both of them still flicking through the pamphlet.

These were the Green and Webster reps, the younger being trained to take over from the older.

"Your numbers are good," Bernie said, flicking through the papers. "But I'm not sure about your growth projections. Kurt?"

The younger guy leaned back in his chair, his teeth flashing as he grinned. "Based on the industry projections at the presentation yesterday, I'd say Annie's underselling her potential."

The older guy made a humming sound under his breath, his fingers running over the page.

I sat at the table, knitting my hands together. "Bernie, Kurt, I'm going to level with you. Green and Webster have long been supporters of eco-friendly options. Your target market is my target market. What do you need from me to make this happen?"

They exchanged a look.

"The three-ply recycled," Bernie said, tapping the pamphlet. "If we did a two year trial, what's the best that you could do?"

I performed mental calculations. "I could cut five percent off for the life of the pilot. But in two years when we renegotiate, you'll need to pay the same price as everyone else."

He crossed his arms. "When we renegotiate? Cocky, aren't you."

"The numbers never lie."

He grinned. "I like your gumption. You got a deal." He held out his hand and I took it, relishing the sweet taste of victory.

"Kurt will send you the contract this week."

"I look forward to it."

We chatted then I guided them to the door, closing it firmly behind them.

Ensuring I was alone and no one could see into the closed meeting room—I fist pumped the air, dipping into a victory dance. As I boogied around the room, I slid a hand into the pocket of my skirt, pulling out a handful of paper confetti to throw in the air.

"Fuck yes!"

I danced under the slowly drifting confetti, laughing as the small paper settled in my hair and on my clothes.

Everyone, I'd long ago decided, needed confetti in their life.

I picked up my phone, dialing my deputy director.

"Any takers?" Sheena asked, disposing of all pleasantries.

"Two," I squealed, gleefully, kicking off my heels. "Green and Webster, and Farm to Table."

"Oh my God! Annie, this is huge!" I heard her fumble with the phone. "Just a minute. Sorry, I have to go. Are you coming back to the stall?"

I'd forked out a lot of money for us to have our own booth at the trade show.

"Yeah, I'll grab us all some lunch first. Text me your orders."

"Will do. Congrats again, can't wait to celebrate with you." She ended the call, and I tossed my phone on the table, allowing myself one last squeal.

Excitement, anticipation, and anxiety rolled in my gut as I slumped in my chair, the stress of the last few hours slowly easing.

"Now we have it all," I whispered. "Nothing can stop us."

On a satisfied sigh, I did the socially responsible thing and bent to pick up all the confetti, storing it in my pocket for future use.

CHAPTER FIVE

Linc

"Dɪᴅ ʏᴏᴜ ᴋɴᴏᴡ," Theo said, looking down at the map in his hand. "There's a toilet here that they brought over from England for the conference. Some old king used it."

I rolled my eyes. "We're not here for toilets. We're here for—"

"Paper products. I know." He paused. "But since we're here...."

I cocked an eyebrow at my brother. "You really want to see where a king took a shit?"

He shrugged. "Why not? Not like we're gonna be able to afford vacations overseas anytime soon."

I hated that he was right.

"Which way are paper products?"

He consulted the map. "Basically that entire quadrant." He pointed to one of the corners of the giant convention center.

I blinked then blinked again. "Shit."

"Yep. That's why we're here." He clapped a hand on my shoulder. "Shit, poop, pee—it's all gonna bring us some money."

"We hope."

"We certainly do. So, plan of attack?"

I eyed the stalls. "Let's do some reconnaissance first—feel out who's looking at recycled options."

"Sounds good."

We made our way down the various alleys, accepting information packs and swag, making small talk with reps who were more than happy to discuss their manufacturing and supply chains.

After lawfully finalizing the power of attorney, Theo and I had spent the last week applying for government grants, renegotiating mortgages and payments, and calling every current, former, and prospective client we could to drum up business.

We'd find out by the end of the month if we were approved for the recycling grant, but in the meantime, we needed to find new clients—stat. When Theo had stumbled across the convention, it had seemed serendipitous. But after talking to half the vendors, I couldn't feel anything but low-grade panic.

"Well fuck me," Theo muttered, tucking another individually wrapped toilet roll into his branded bag. "I'm never gonna need to shop for swag again."

My gut churned. "No one needs a manufacturer. The ones that might be a good fit are all established, and the start-ups need someone who can meet small numbers. Even if we managed to sign all the start-ups here, we'd still be a few hundred thousand short of what we need." I ran a hand over my face. "Fuck me. We're gonna lose the business."

My brother lifted the convention map waving it in front of my face. "There are still thirty-odd vendors on this list. Surely at least one is a medium-to-large enterprise looking for a company ready to bend over backwards for their business."

"Let's fucking hope."

We continued down the alleys, Theo's good humor waning as we spoke to company after company, none of them interested in a new manufacturer.

"Last five," he said, as we left the Green Waste stall. "Fuck I hope there's someone in this mix."

I nodded, determined to find at least one contact.

"Where to first?"

I jerked my head toward a stall with a giant recycle symbol. "Let's try that one."

It looked more like a bar than a trade booth, the colorful pops of individually wrapped toilet paper adding to the festive atmosphere.

"Who's this?" I asked, impressed with the layout.

"Shit Happens," Theo read. "Why does that sound familiar?"

I blinked. "Did you say—?"

"I'll be with you in one second," a familiar voice called. "Feel free to look around."

I twisted, finding a very familiar, very perfect ass pointed straight at me. The woman rummaging in her bag, muttering to herself – her hair falling in a magnificent curtain down her back.

Fuck.

I knew that ass. I knew that head of fucking magnificent hair. I'd kissed those legs and the three freckles behind her left knee.

Fuck. Fuck. Fuck!

I began to backpedal, attempting to avoid detection but to no avail. As if in slow motion, Annie stood, golden hair flying in an impressive arch as she turned, a welcoming smile lighting her face.

Fuck, she looked incredible. Black heels, skintight skirt that showed off all her curves, a professional blouse with her S#!t Happens logo embroidered on her breast. My fingers itched to rip it apart, revealing her ample curves hidden beneath.

Hey, dickhead. This is your ex, remember?

Her smile felt like being touched by the fucking sun —and just as quickly it banked, her eyes narrowing, the glow shuttered.

"You."

I crossed my arms, fucking pissed she'd tossed me back into the shadows. "Yep, it's me."

"What are you doing here?"

"Same as everyone else, I imagine." I held up one of my goodie bags. "Market research."

"You aren't in sanitation."

"Yet," I corrected.

"Never. Your father made that extremely clear five years ago."

I exchanged a glance with Theo, seeing my confusion reflected back.

"What do you mean?"

Annie crossed her arms, leaning back against the bar.

"Toilet paper," she said, her tone faintly mocking. "Is not worthy of the Garrett name."

"Yeah, that sounds like something the old fucker would say," Theo muttered darkly.

"Walter's not in charge of the business anymore."

Her eyebrows shot up, some of her righteous anger fading. "I heard about his accident. I'm sorry. I didn't realize it was that bad."

"Oh, it's bad." Theo reached for one of the beers in the middle of the table. "These free?"

Annie nodded, her gaze dancing from me to him and back again. "So, you're running Garrett Paper now?"

"Yep." I cocked an eyebrow. "Just like you always said would happen."

She smiled tightly.

"You're not after a manufacturer by any chance?" Theo dropped a second beer into his bag.

"No. But even if I was," her gaze locked with mine. "I wouldn't go with you."

"Because of Walter?" Theo asked.

She dropped her gaze, glancing away.

"Sure. Because of him."

Liar.

"What if we made you an offer?" I asked. "Worked out a better deal than your current supplier?"

She stared at me then turned retreated, giving me her back. "No, thank you. But try the Harding team two stalls down. They're looking to expand."

Theo grinned, gathering his stash of promotional merch. "Thanks, Annie. You're the best."

She lifted her head in acknowledgement but didn't move. As Theo strolled from the booth, I waited, willing her to look at me. I wanted her to acknowledge the ghosts between us.

Her hands gripped the bar top, her knuckles white.

"Annie, I—"

An attendee strode into the booth, breaking our stale mate.

"Wow," he said, glancing around. "This is cool."

And just like that, Annie pulled herself together, a mask slipping into place. "Welcome, I'm Annie, CEO and Founder of Shit Happens. Can I get you a drink?"

I watched for a beat longer, my head now as fucked up as my heart.

"Did you know about Dad?" Theo asked when I caught up to him.

"Fuck no. Did you?"

He shook his head. "Fucking idiot. Annie's going places. He's a fool to have not seen it."

"He never saw it. Not once."

Theo shot me a look. "What's that supposed to mean?"

"Nothing." I pointed to the Harding stall. "Better get your game face on."

"Linc?"

I glanced at my brother.

"We're gonna talk about this later."

I grunted.

"I'm serious."

I rolled my shoulders trying to throw off some of the

weight that had settled on them. "Let's deal with the business first. We can talk about feelings and shit later."

"Fine." My brother waggled a finger at me. "But we will be talking about it."

I made a noncommittal sound.

Over my dead body.

CHAPTER SIX

Annie

My closet consisted of eight pairs of jeans, twelve shirts with S#!T Happens logos, two dozen shirts with various amusing puns, three dresses—one for funerals, one for weddings, and one for dates—one business skirt. Not to mention copious amounts of what I liked to call 'workout clothing' and but wore while watching Netflix and eating ice cream from a carton.

The one thing I didn't own?

A goddamned Kevlar vest. But fuck if I didn't need one right now. Between Linc wandering around the convention, my manufacturer dodging my calls, and the death glares from my competition, I felt like I should be donning some kind of protection.

"I'm back." Sheena plucked a to-go cup from the cardboard tray, offering me a pick me up.

"Bless you," I praised, lifting the coffee to my nose taking a long inhale. "Mm, bliss."

"Did I miss anything?"

I glanced around the mostly empty booth, noting our other staff were chatting with a smaller vendor.

Short and fierce, with pale skin and dark almost-black hair, Sheena looked like a pint-sized goth—except for her tendency to wear loud colors. She may lack the fierce Irish temper of her siblings, but a better director I couldn't ask for. We'd met in college, the only two women in our statistics course. We'd bonded over misogynism and standard deviation. When I'd started S#!T Happens, Sheena had been the first to put her hand up and assist. After the first three months I'd been able to start paying her. Within six, we'd had official titles, salaried income, and an actual office. I'd be lost without her.

I dropped my voice, moving closer to Sheena.

"Well, my ex and his brother stopped by the stall. A guy from Jarvis Industry offered to buy the company for a million dollars—don't worry," I said, catching her flare of outrage. "I educated him quick smart."

"Good."

"Colton is still dodging my calls." I ticked off the final items on my fingers. "And Chester from Blue Pad stopped by to hint that they were in discussions with him." I took a sip of the coffee, relishing the rich taste as it hit my tongue. "Yeah, I'd say you missed a few things."

"Oh, dear," she murmured, her dark eyes wide. "I'm not sure where to start."

"I think the implied threat from our competition that he might be trying to poach our manufacturer would be the priority."

"Ah. So, about that...."

I stared down at her. "Sheena, what do you know?"

She danced from foot to foot. "Nothing. Well, something. No, it's probably nothing. It's just—"

"Jesus, woman. Spit it out."

"I saw Colton and Chester talking in the VIP lounge," she burst out, her sentences flowing together in a jumble. "I thought it was weird but didn't think it was a big deal so ended up just getting our coffees and coming back. But now you've said something, I wonder if it really is *something*, you know?"

"That motherfucker." I gritted my teeth. "He knows I've put all the work in to get Colton up to standard and now he's gonna try and poach him? Fuck that."

"Surely not."

I straightened my skirt, an unholy rage burning in my gut.

"Don't you remember Rineheart?"

Sheena winced, adjusting her glasses. "Fuck. How could I forget?"

Rinehart had been our previous manufacturer. In our first year they'd helped us grow the business, only to sell out to Chester when Blue Pad came knocking. As a result, prices went up while quality went down—leaving us with no choice but to move to another manufacturer.

"Surely you're not thinking he'll do it again?" Sheena said, watching me fix my hair in one of the mirrors lining the side of the bar.

"I wouldn't put anything past Chester. Or Colton, for that matter. The both of them know they have me over a barrel—and what's better than forcing someone to pay more for the same product?"

"Having a monopoly on the product. Shit."

I nodded. "VIP lounge you said?"

Sheena grimaced. "Yeah. Are you sure you want to do this?"

"If they've got nothing to hide then I'm sure this will be a collegial chat."

"And if they do?"

I shot her a deadly grin. "I'll cross that bridge when I come to it."

I left my team behind at the booth, weaving through the convention center toward the back of the giant auditorium. A VIP room had been set up down the hall from the trade room, giving stall holders a quiet area to eat food and drink, and to hold meetings as required.

I walked into the café-style room, my gaze narrowing on Chester and Colton across the room. Papers were spread in front of them, both signing documents.

"Over my dead body," I muttered.

Sheena's voice sounded in my head. *Calm. Give them the benefit of the doubt.*

"Gentlemen," I greeted, stopping in front of their table. "How lovely to see you both."

Hands fumbled, gathering the papers as they stuttered out hellos.

Well, that answers some of my questions.

"Annie." Chester stood, stepping neatly in front of the table, blocking my view. "Can I get you coffee?"

Chester Gordon had inherited Blue Pad from his uncle. Ruthlessly efficient, he'd set about turning it into one of the biggest recycling paper companies in America. At first, I'd admired him, aspiring to be like the handsome, young CEO—then I'd read the reports. Blue Pad's environmental promises were as cheap as the paper they'd been printed on. Chester didn't care about the environment, he prized the few extra dollars anything with a green tick could bring.

"No." I looked over his shoulder at Colton. "I was looking for Mr. Davis, actually. I wanted to talk numbers for the next quarter."

Colton Davis looked like a stereotypical grandfather —jolly beard, giant beer gut, ruddy cheeks. But under his unassuming exterior lurked a shark.

He cleared his throat. "Chester and I were just finishing."

I glanced at Chester. "Fortuitous timing on my part."

A muscle in Chester's jaw twitched. "I'll leave you to it." He held out a hand to Colton. "Mr. Davis, we'll be in touch."

I took Chester's abandoned seat, knitting my hands together on the table as I watched Colton gather the papers.

Pauses, I'd learned, made people uncomfortable. Colton was no different.

"He's offered me a better deal."

I arched an eyebrow.

"No change in current practices, more money." The older man lifted his hands in a 'what can you do' gesture. "Between the two of you—his offer wins."

I pressed my lips together, my stomach beginning to gurgle, the sound and sensation only too familiar.

Fuck. Not now.

"What are you saying?" I asked him, praying my gut

wouldn't choose that moment to begin what I called its whale chorus.

Crohn's disease—what a pain in the ass.

"Unless you want to pay more and agree to drop your crusade to get that fancy certification, we're done."

"Being B Corp Certified assists us to get to the next level. Without the certification we're not demonstrating a true point of difference—or a commitment to what we're preaching."

He shrugged, crossing his arms over his chest. "Those are my terms."

I swallowed, a familiar pinching-kick beginning on the right side of my upper abdomen.

Not now. Come on body. Not now.

"You're not willing to negotiate?"

He shook his head.

I stood, forcing myself to ignore the cramps ripping through my gut. My hands curled into fists, my fingernails digging into my palm in an effort to hold myself upright.

Don't show weakness.

"Then we'll finish out our contract."

"You have sixty days."

I stared at him, nausea joining the pain. " The contract isn't due for renewal until the end of the year."

"True. But the clause includes a provision for me to give you a sixty-day notice of termination if you didn't meet our terms during the renegotiation period." He pushed up from the table, gathering his things. "Consider this your sixty days' notice."

"You can't do that."

"You gonna meet my terms?"

I shook my head slowly, sweat beading my brow.

"Then we have nothing left to discuss. Martha will send you the details of the wrap up next week. Have a good conference, Annie."

I watched him leave, catching sight of the last person I ever wanted to see.

Lincoln.

"Enjoy the show?" I asked, forcing steel into my spine, determined to remain strong.

"Are you alright?" He glanced back at Colton. "That sounded—"

My stomach lurched, a familiar, awful, watery sensation hitting my bowels, my situation had just become dire.

"Fine," I barked, hunching slightly as I headed for the bathroom. "Mind your own business, Lincoln. From what I hear, it needs all the help it can get."

I managed to make it inside the accessible stall before giving in to the pain, folding in on myself.

"Fuck," I groaned, hugging my middle. "Fuck, fuck, fuck!"

In my rush to stop Colton and Chester, I'd left my tote in the booth. Doubled over with pain, I shoved my skirt up and underwear down, death-gripping the support bars on either side of the toilet, gingerly lowering myself to the seat.

"Fuck," I groaned, my eyes squeezing shut, my body tearing itself in two. "Fuck, fuck, fuck!"

I pulled my phone from my pocket, typing out a quick text.

Annie: SOS. Can you bring my bag? I need the Colofac and heat patches in the front pocket. I'm in the accessible toilet in the VIP lounge. Hurry, please!

Sheena: Awww, babe. I'm on it!

"Talk about the day going to shit." I closed my eyes, letting out a long, low groan. Cramps wracked my body, the pain familiar and overwhelming.

"Annie?" There was a soft tap on the stall door. "You in there?"

"Yep," I called, my voice weak. "Can you throw my bag in?"

"Sure."

The door cracked open a fraction, my tote sliding across the grimy tiles.

Fuck. Too far away.

I leaned over, one hand death gripping a support bar, the other stretched out to try and hook a finger under a shoulder strap.

"Fuck. Come here you mother—gotcha." I dragged it to me, heaving it onto my lap to dig through—pausing when a new, intense wave of cramping hit my gut.

"Oh, God."

"Are you okay in there?" Sheena called anxiously.

No. Not even close.

"Fine," I lied. "Just a little cramping. Give me ten minutes and it'll be fine."

I popped the pills and pulled a disposable heat pack free, peeling off the plastic backing to stick over my abdomen.

"Fucking, fuck, fuck." I groaned, doubling over. With one hand pressed tight to my stomach, I fumbled with the toilet paper dispenser, my fingers meeting cardboard tube.

"You have got to be shitting me. No paper? We're at a toilet convention!"

I pulled a spare roll from my bag, feeling a strange sense of déjà vu.

Bent over, pain ratcheting through my body, I stared blankly at the empty toilet roll dispenser, transported back to the day I'd decided to create S#!T Happens.

This felt like a sign from the universe—good or bad, I wasn't yet sure.

"This won't be our end," I promised fiercely. "This is just the beginning."

CHAPTER SEVEN

Linc

THE HOST of the trade show certainly knew how to put on a party. An open bar, delicious finger food, and great music almost had me relaxing.

Almost. Afterall, how relaxed could you be when the fate of two hundred employees rested on your shoulders?

Theo and I had spent the night mingling, rubbing elbows with distributors, manufacturers, producers, and suppliers—none of whom seemed to need paper from a failing mill.

But then someone had referred us to Colton Davis—the King of Sanitation.

"I know your father." The older man licked barbeque sauce from his fingertips. "Good guy that Walter."

I exchanged a look with Theo.

"And how do you know our dear old dad?" My brother asked, playing the dopey ne'er-do-well. "Old college roommates?"

Colton chuckled, his white beard stained with sauce. "Something like that. Shame to hear about his accident."

I cleared my throat. "Yeah. Real shame. It's actually why we're here, we're trying to pivot the business."

Colton's bushy eyebrows rose. "Really? That's a surprise. Last I heard your daddy wasn't one for change."

Theo laughed, clapping a hand on his shoulder. "Ain't that the truth?"

The older man lifted his beer, turning it slowly in his hands.

"Word has it, you boys need some contracts to stay afloat."

I tensed. "Word would be right."

He nodded, taking a long, slow pull of his beer.

Theo glanced at me, shifting his weight from side-to-side.

"You ever think of selling?" Colton asked.

I tried for casual. "It's a family business, we don't sell."

"Everybody's got a price." He reached for the bowl of chicken wings in the middle of the table, taking his time selecting his next mouthful.

"Not us."

The older man chuckled, tearing into the wing. "You don't strike me as the type of boys to turn a good offer down. I'll tell it to you straight—your warehouse is in a distribution location I want. I'll give you a fair price. With the kind of money I'm offering, you'll both be able to live very comfortable lives."

He caught Theo's frown. "Well, hell—you want to stay on? I can make that happen too. How does a management position sound?"

Theo shook his head slowly. "We're after clients—not a corporate takeover."

"What choice do you have? You're late to the party." He waved a hand at the room. "You're fighting an uphill battle to get clients. This is the ocean, boys. And you're living in a backwater swamp."

I gritted my teeth.

Colton rubbed a hand down his front, leaving behind a smear of chicken grease. "How about I name a price and you nod?"

"That's not—"

He interrupted, naming an amount that involved a shit-ton of zeroes. I felt Theo wavering, the offer seemingly too good to be true.

Across the bar I caught a flash of golden hair.

Colton's confrontation with Annie had stuck with me. She'd lashed out when I'd asked, but I'd caught the flash of vulnerability in her expression before she had hidden it away.

Treat your employees and clients like they're family, and they'll be loyal to you.

My grandfather's voice whispered in my ear, the unsettled feeling in my gut building.

"I saw you this afternoon," I said lightly, watching Colton closely for his reaction. "In the VIP lounge you were talking with Annie Harris. Is she a client?"

"Not for long." He tossed the cleaned bones onto the table, lifting another wing from the basket. "Fussiest bitch I've ever met."

"Hey," I snapped. "Inappropriate."

The old man's brow creased, his eyes narrowing

before a façade of pleasantness settled over his features. "You're right. My apologies."

He gestured at a passing waiter, ordering us another round. My concerns grew as the night matured, Colton's sly digs and veiled criticisms giving way to a mean streak the longer he drank.

Done with the man, I stood, stepping away from the table. "Thanks for the chat. I'm gonna head to bed."

Colton stopped me. "You selling me the mill, Lincoln? Or will you let her die a slow death?"

"Thanks for the offer, but Garrett Paper isn't for sale." I lifted my beer bottle in a mocking toast. "Have a good night, Mr. Davis."

I walked away, hearing him lay into Theo, demanding my brother fix this.

Over my dead body.

I left the bar, walking through the quiet lobby, my mind whirling.

Is she a client?

Not for long.

I shoved through the convention center doors and out into the quiet night. Discarding my beer bottle, I tucked my hands in my pockets, needing a long walk to bring clarity to my turbulent thoughts.

Not for long.

Not for long.

Not for long.

Colton's words looped, an idea beginning to take root.

"Don't be fucking stupid," I muttered, stopping to stare up at the moon. "If you were smart, you'd get off your moral high horse, go back, and accept Colton's offer."

Ration and logic said he'd be the safe choice—but the way he'd spoken about Annie rubbed me the wrong way.

"Fuck." I pinched the bridge of my nose. "Don't be an idiot."

My idea—one born of desperation and hope took shape.

"She's gonna hate it," I muttered to myself, starting back for the hotel.

A dark voice offered a suggestion.

Make it worth her while.

"Fuck."

I knew what I had to do—I just hoped I wasn't about to make the worst decision of my life.

CHAPTER EIGHT

Annie

"It feels as if life has no meaning," I bemoaned, my forehead pressed to the table.

Around me, the house buzzed with friends and family, the smell of sweat and beer hung heavy in the air —the odors adding to my despair.

Every Friday night someone in our friendship group hosted a Friday Feast. We rotated around the group—this week it was Ren, Mai's brother's turn. He'd organized a Korean-Japanese rib infusion that had tasted phenomenal.

But no matter how amazing the food, how great the company, or how good the beer—I couldn't shake the feeling that my world was ending.

"I take it Annie's at the existential-crisis part of her drunk cycle?" Flo commented, returning to her seat at the table, Ace, her guide dog, settling beside her.

It'd been three weeks since Colton had offered his

ultimatum, and I still hadn't found a manufacturer willing to meet my standards.

"Mm," Mai murmured, picking at the label of her beer. "And a good one at that."

"I hate you both." I propped my chin on my hands, staring at her morosely. "You're so mean to me."

Tonight, Mai had channeled her inner punk—clothing herself in an outfit of her own design. She'd handcrafted the leather jacket with its studs and patches over the past year, and when coupled with the faded wash jeans and a vintage band t-shirt, she looked ready to take to the stage. Not that she would, the woman hated being the center of attention.

"You know," she said, reaching out to brush crumbs from my cheek. "There's a Japanese proverb my mother would trot out at a time like this—wake from death and return to life."

"And that means?"

"Stop being a dickhead and turn your situation around."

Flo sighed, her fingers beginning to unwrap her brunette braid. "You should be kinder to Annie—she's obviously had a bad day."

More like a bad month.

I caught one of her hands, squeezing her elegant fingers. "Thank you, my darling."

With her delicate features and tendency to wear soft, flowy fabrics, Flo reminded me of a fairy princess awaiting her prince.

"If Frankie were here, she'd tell you to pick yourself up, dust yourself off, and get on with it."

"Alas, Frankie is fucking her fiancé." I giggled. "Try saying that five times."

"I need another beer. This is getting ridiculous." Mai hauled herself up from the table, her lips thinning when she spotted the seething mass of bodies surrounding the kitchen. "On second thought, do we really need another round? Or are you sufficiently drunk enough to leave?"

I waved a hand in her direction. "Can one be 'sufficiently drunk' if one is still walking?"

Ace huffed from his spot beside Flo's chair.

"See?" I pointed at the golden lab. "He gets it."

"*He* is tired and ready for me to go home," Flo corrected.

I glanced at my watch, squinting as I tried to read the numbers. "Shit. It's late."

"Yep. So unless you want to tell us exactly why you've kept us from our beauty sleep, I think we'll call it a night." Flo started to rise, Mai reaching for her tote.

Desperate to avoid being alone with my depressing thoughts, I blew out a noisy breath.

"Sit your asses down. I'll tell you."

A toxic mix of emotions churned in my stomach, the acid brew burning up my throat.

"My supplier isn't renewing our contract. I have sixty-days—or, more precisely, thirty-eight days, to find a new manufacturer or Shit Happens is finished."

"Fuck."

"Oh, Annie."

I scrubbed a hand over my face. "No one who can meet our standards is taking on new clients. I've called every manufacturer from here to Australia which means we either compromise on our product or—" I choked, a sob catching in my throat.

"Or?" Mai asked, one hand gently rubbing circles across my back.

I shook my head, unable to give the words a voice.

"What if you became a manufacturer?" Flo asked. "Is that hard? I know it would be expensive but surely in the long term it would be a good investment."

I sighed. "It's not that easy. And not in the time I need. We'd need supply contracts for recycled paper, we'd need to set up manufacturing. I'd have to fork out for machinery and recruitment and—"

"Right," Flo huffed out a laugh. "Stupid suggestion."

"Not stupid, just not feasible. If I had a year, I'd definitely explore it. I'm done being screwed over. This is my life. This is my company. I—" The trapped sob tore free.

"Oh, Annie."

Arms wrapped around me, holding me tight.

"I'm okay," I assured them, scrubbing at my tears. "I'm fine."

"You're not. And that's okay. This is a shitty situation."

And now comes the hard part.

"I got a letter today. I might have a third option."

They sat back, waiting for me to continue.

"Lincoln wrote to me."

"Lincoln as in Garrett?" Flo asked, her forehead creasing.

"Yeah." I closed my eyes. "He's offering me a fifty-percent share in Garrett Paper."

The plain envelope had held the answers to all my prayers—but came attached to my worst nightmare.

"Heaven and hell," I whispered. "Who invites their ex-girlfriend to become a business partner?"

Mai frowned. "You'd really say no to this opportunity? You'd let an ex stand between you and the success of your company?" She flicked a finger against my forehead. "Priorities, Annie."

"I can't disassociate myself from our past." Pain cut deep at the thought of bringing Linc back into my life.

"Why not?" Flo asked, brushing fingers through my hair. "He's just a man you used to know."

"He's not," I admitted, finally giving words to the truth of our past. "He's never been just a man I used to know." I sucked in a breath, fighting tears.

Flo reached out to Mai, their hands squeezing mine.

"You wonder why I struggle when I see him? It's because this town—it feels like a memorial to a war we lost." I knew I sounded crazy but the words kept flowing. I shook my head. "He understood me. He loved me."

"Oh, Annie...."

I brushed at a stray tear. "This whole goddamn town is a memory bomb waiting to detonate—walking down Main Street, swimming in the ocean, checking a book out at the library. Every movement, every action, every place is tied to him. You guys wonder why I hate seeing him? Why I get so distraught and annoyed every time?"

My chest hitched, my throat tight.

"It's because I'm left shell-shocked—shattered and broken every single *fucking* time. I don't have any answers to why he broke up with me. It still fucking hurts. It breaks me a little every time cause after every glimpse and memory I'm left asking the same fucking question—why? What was it that made me not good enough? Why did he discard me when everything up to that point had been nothing but promises of forever?"

I swallowed, looking down at my hands, the anger fading to leave behind a familiar, throbbing ache.

"It hurts."

Two sets of arms wrapped around me, holding me tight as I shattered, my shoulders heaving with silent sobs.

"You're good enough. You're better than good enough," Mai whispered fiercely. "You're perfect. So, fucking perfect. You can't doubt yourself like this. You can't place your worth in his hands."

I wanted to tell them my greatest fear. I wanted to release it from the dark place within me, but the words wouldn't come—sticking in my throat, my mouth opening to release a screaming silence.

Did he dump me because I'm a burden?

"He didn't deserve you." Flo pressed a kiss to my damp cheek. "You deserve someone who'll give you the world."

"The problem is," I whispered, resting my head on her shoulder. "I had it. I had someone who gave me everything. Every part of himself. Every part of me. And he took it away."

Flo let me go, leaning back in her chair. "Is he why you left?"

I paused. "Yes." I admitted. "The memories were too painful. You have to understand, I tried. I tried to get over him. I dated, I fell into relationships, but always—always

—he was there, in the back of my mind like some kind of terrible poltergeist."

"He's your Captain Wentworth," Flo whispered, her hands pressing to her heart.

"What?"

She tipped her head to one side, her locks falling off her shoulder. "Well, more precisely you're *his* Captain Wentworth. Which makes him your Anne."

I exchanged a bewildered glance with Mai. "What are you talking about?"

"Persuasion by Jane Austen. Haven't you read it? Or watched any of the movies?"

"No? Should I?"

She nodded. "Go home right now and find it. The 1995 version is the best but—"

I began to laugh, tears streaming down my cheeks.

"Trust you to want to romanticize this moment."

Her hand slid across the table, finding my arm. Gently, she glided her palm up, following the line of my body until she could cup my cheek.

"If your heart still loves him, if your soul still wants him, then maybe you need to allow it to do so. That love doesn't need to be romantic, Annie. But if he is your other half, maybe this is the universe's way of bringing you back together to heal. Friendship is just as important as romantic love."

I glanced at Mai, finding her staring at Flo.

"Well, damn," she whispered. "That's profound."

I snorted, breaking the mood. "You're both crazy."

Flo dropped her hand, her fingers slowly gliding

across the table as she located her beer. "Crazy? Or crazy smart?"

"What are you going to do?" Mai brought the conversation back to the issue at hand.

I closed my eyes, pinching the bridge of my nose. "I don't know yet."

We sat quietly, ignoring the laughter of the house party around us.

"Shots?" Flo asked.

"Shots," I agreed.

"Stay here." She shoved up from the table. "I know where Ren keeps his liquor stash. Be right back."

I watched her walk away, Ace guiding her from the room as I tried to talk myself out of what I knew I needed to do.

"You're going to speak to Linc, aren't you?" Mai asked, picking at the label on her empty beer bottle.

"You're both right. I need to move on." I sighed. "Whatever we had is dead. My company isn't. If this is what I need to do to grow, then so be it."

Mai nodded, her giant hoop earrings brushing her shoulder. "Frankie's gonna be pissed she missed this little convo. The great Annie finally admitting she has a soft belly?" She shook her head, her eyes sparkling. "She'll demote you to bridesmaid."

I chuckled. "How's her dress coming?"

Mai's gaze turned dreamy. "It's perfect for her. I can't wait for you guys to see it."

"When will it be ready?"

"Soon, I hope. I thought we could do a fitting at red and read night in a few weeks for the grand reveal."

"Perfect." I raised my beer. "To Frankie and Jay, a perfect match."

Mai hesitated, then clinked her glass against mine. "To beautiful love stories—no matter what form they take."

We both drank deep.

"You want some chocolate?" Mai pulled a giant block from her bag.

"Fucking always."

Over cheap tequila, lots of chocolate, and gentle ribbing, I began to see a light at the end of the dark tunnel.

CHAPTER NINE

Linc

THE SINGLE PIECE of paper taunted me from its spot on the desk. The size fourteen, double-spaced font could be read from each corner of the room.

Colleagues,

It is with the greatest sadness that Theo and I have made the difficult decision to place Garrett Paper for sale.

"You sure about this?" Theo asked. "There's absolutely no other option?"

"Only one, and it's a long shot."

My brother looked like shit—and I had no doubt I looked the same. Dark circles under his eyes, his hair overly long and mussed, he looked as exhausted as I felt.

We'd busted our asses for the last few weeks, working all hours, bending over backwards to find a way out of the hole Walter had put us in.

The few additional contracts we'd managed to secure weren't enough to keep the business afloat—and they certainly weren't enough to impress the bank or the government. We'd been denied both grants and loans.

"If you can prove you're viable," the sympathetic government representative had said on the rejection call. "Then we'd invite you to resubmit. Your application was excellent, it just lacked proof of sustained income."

I downed the rest of my coffee, grimacing when the cold brew hit my tongue.

"We have no choice." I discarded my mug. "We need to give people notice."

"Some will stay in town."

I nodded.

"But the rest?" Theo slumped against the filing cabinet, his head dropping. "You ever feel like a failure?"

"Every fucking day."

We exchanged a bittersweet smile.

"You sure you don't want to take Colton's offer?"

I shook my head. "He's not right for this company. When we sell, we'll need to do right by our people. They're the only ones who matter now."

We fell silent.

"So, this is it. The day Garrett Paper dies."

I scrubbed a hand over my face. "Yep."

"We did our best, Lincoln."

"Pity it wasn't enough."

Theo swirled his mug absently.

"What if we ask Mom again? Surely she could see the value of—"

"No." I killed his hope. "She made it clear she wasn't an option."

On hands and knees, I'd castrated myself before my

mother, begging her for a loan. Eleanor Partridge wasn't the motherly type. A cut-throat politician, our mother had spent most of our formative years in Washington, working her way up the political ladder.

"Said it would be a conflict of interest."

"Saving two hundred jobs from certain extinction in her own electorate is a conflict?"

I swallowed the impotent rage burning in my gut. "She said it was market forces at work and we should be grateful to have an opportunity to move on with our lives."

Theo swore softly. "We really scraped the bottom of the supportive parent barrel."

I stared down at my speech, mentally bracing myself for what was to come.

The clock on the wall inched closer to nine-thirty, the sound overly loud in the quiet of our office.

"You ready?" Theo asked.

I shook my head, pushing to a stand. "Can you ever be?"

He crossed the room, pulling me in for a tight, back-clapping hug. "We'll get through this. You're right—we're doing what's best for our workers."

And that was the only fucking bright side of this mess.

"Alright." I shoved him away, smoothing my Garrett Paper polo. "Don't get too emotional on me. We can double shot a whiskey later. Let's just get through the next half-hour."

A knock stopped us, the door opening to reveal the last person I'd ever thought to see.

Holy shit. She came.

"Annie." Her name tasted sweet on my tongue.

Her golden gaze flicked from me to Theo. "Do you two have a few minutes? I have something I'd like to discuss with you." She held up a familiar manilla envelope.

Fuck.

"Of course." I gestured at her to take a seat. "Come on in."

She entered the room and I took my first, real look at her in nearly a decade.

I watched her glide across the room, her body poetry in motion. From the dance of the strands of her hair escaping her ponytail, to the purse of her painted red lips, and down to the sway of her jean-clad hips—every part of her whispered of hot, dirty nights, and long, lazy mornings with my face buried between her legs. I wanted to kiss the lipstick from her lips, and hear her needy pants and loving moans as she shattered under my hands.

I stuffed the speech in a drawer as she settled on the other side of the desk, resting her hands on the chipped laminate top, her golden gaze considering.

Theo boosted onto the shelving unit behind me, his prosthetic thumping gently against the shelving in time with his leg swing.

Bump, bump, bump.

"I read your proposal." She tossed the envelope on the desk between us. "I accept."

Theo's legs stopped bouncing.

I locked my hands together, forcing calm.

"Accept what, exactly?"

Annie's steely gaze reminded me of a lioness stalking her prey. "The partnership offer."

"Fifty-fifty?" I asked, my tone neutral.

She tapped a finger on the envelope. "Signed, sealed, and delivered."

I exhaled, my shoulders relaxing. "Any changes to my offer?"

A smug grin teased at the corners of her mouth. "Open it and see."

CHAPTER TEN

Annie

I WATCHED the emotions play across Linc's face as he read the adjustments in the contract.

I'd thought long and hard about what to say to explain my change of mind. His proposal had been unexpected and—at first—hurtful. I'd raged, and ranted, spending hours creating speeches and rehearsing words that felt raw, and wrong, and full of nothing but piss and vinegar.

They didn't call me dramatic for nothing.

But after speaking to Mai and Flo, I'd put aside the hurts of the past, and looked at what he offered —a true partnership.

"What made you change your mind?" he asked.

This would be the part I hated, being forced to eat humble pie.

"I want to have control of my company from start to finish." I laid myself out, exposing my vulnerable belly.

"I'm tired of being reliant on men who don't care about what I'm working to achieve. No one will care about your business as much as you do, and I care. I care so fucking much that I can't stand to not be in charge of all aspects." I pointed to the contract. "You have the machinery, skill, and talent, I have the funds and vision. You're right. This is an opportunity that benefits both of us."

Linc watched me with his dark eyes, his brow furrowed. I recognized his look, my tension easing.

He's going to say yes.

"We're broke."

The words landed between us with all the grace of a hippo.

"Jesus, Linc!" Theo threw his arms up. "You don't tell her that. You accept the fucking offer."

Linc ignored him, his gaze locked with mine.

"If we're lucky, we've got two months left." He reached into his drawer, pulling out a sheet of paper.

I took it, reading his speech to his employees.

"Walter?" I asked.

He nodded once, his expression dark.

"Have you told them yet?" I placed the sheet on the desk, smoothing it with trembling fingers.

"We were on our way to deliver it when you walked in."

I looked down at the paper. "Why did you tell me? Why not hide it?"

"You deserve to know what you're tying yourself to. And to present you with a different option."

My head tilted back, my gaze crashing into his.

"A different option?"

"We'll sell the mill to you, if you want it."

He looked stoic, emotionless, but I caught the tension in his hands, the flick of pain in his gaze.

He cares. He wants this place to succeed.

My heart did a little skip, a lightness settling in my chest. He could have lied and gotten what he wanted, instead here he sat, laying it all on the line.

Fuck. I hate that I respect him.

"I want the partnership. 50-50." I held out a hand for him to shake. "Will you have me?"

He took my hand, his palm familiar and yet different. New calluses slid against my skin, his large hand holding a man's strength.

"We have a deal," he confirmed, his voice full of emotion.

We let go, and I saw his hand flex, his fingers curling into a fist as if he wanted to savor the feel of my skin for a little longer.

"I'll call Scott," Theo said, sliding from his perch on the shelving. "Get him to look it over."

I nodded, standing. "Right, well. I'll leave you to it. We'll be in touch."

I picked up my things, turning to the door.

"Annie?" Linc's low rumble halted my retreat. I glanced at him over my shoulder, struck by the changes in him. He was no mere boy anymore—this creature before me was all man.

"Yes?" I asked, forcing a lightness I didn't feel into my tone.

"Thank you."

A rush of something indescribable flooded my blood.

"Don't thank me yet," I warned. "You're going to hate working with me."

"I somehow doubt that."

The warm respect in his gaze hit me, an answering flame in my belly.

I turned, bustling toward the exit. "Have your people call mine. All the details are in the envelope." I stopped in the doorway, gesturing at the office. "And the first order of business will be to liven this up. It looks like a morgue in here." I shot them a wink. "Later, boys."

With a determination born of desperation, I fled—albeit, gracefully—Garrett Paper, every step of the way questioning my sanity.

CHAPTER ELEVEN

Linc

BASKETBALL WEDNESDAYS WERE A SACRED TRADITION, only the most serious of reasons were accepted for being absent—though we occasionally moved the date to allow for work commitments.

"In the decade we've been playing," Theo drawled, shooting Jay a mock glare. "Linc and I have missed a total of four games. Two for the flu, one for a death, and the latest thanks to Walter's accident." He tossed the ball at Jay. "A flat tire is not an acceptable reason to be late."

Jay caught it, rolling his eyes. "If it wasn't for the beer, I wouldn't even be here."

"None of us would," Ren said cheerfully, finishing lacing his sneakers. "Though the bragging rights are nice."

"Bro." I clapped him on the shoulder. "You haven't won in months. What bragging rights are you talking about? Biggest loser?"

The games had begun as a way to encourage Theo to

re-engage with his body. Losing his leg had fucked him up—and the prescription medications hadn't helped. He'd been depressed, listless, and freaking me the fuck out. I'd spent nights sitting outside his bedroom door, listening for his breathing, terrified I'd lose him if something didn't change.

Jay—having just returned from two years abroad—had invited us to shoot some hoops. Ren had been using the court at the time, and we'd somehow ended up in a friendly game of horse. It'd been the first time in months I'd seen Theo smile.

As he'd mastered his prosthetic leg, the games had escalated until full-body contact had become the accepted norm.

"Time to put your money where your mouth is, Garrett." Jay darted at Theo, dodging around my brother and sprinting for the far hoop, ball bouncing with his stride. "I'm taking out tonight's top prize."

"You fucking wish." Theo chased him down the court, managing to catch the rebound.

The game carried on, bumps and bruises coupled with the occasional 'unintentional' tripping.

I misjudged a pass, frustrated when Theo pressed his advantage, passing the ball to Ren, Jay chasing him down the court, cursing with every step.

While Theo and I were all bulk—Ren and Jay were tall and lean, adding speed to our respective teams. We played first to seventy points, the losers buying the first round at the bar later.

"Fuck," I groaned, tossing my hands up. "How'd he land that?"

"And that's the game." Ren called, shooting Theo a thumbs up. "I've got a taste for some fine gin tonight."

I exchanged a glance with Jay, the guy smothering a laugh. Our friend wasn't exactly known for his drinking habits. The term lightweight seemed more accurate.

"Since when," I asked drolly. "Do you drink hard liquor?"

Ren lifted one shoulder in a half-shrug. "Flo got me on to it. She's been experimenting with a line of floral gins."

Jay clapped a hand on his shoulder. "Now that I'm marrying into the friendship group—"

"Jesus, Jay." Theo slapped hands over his ears. "Stop with the fucking wedding talk."

"We're gonna have to cut you off," Ren agreed. "You're insufferable."

"You would be too, if you were marrying the sexiest woman in the world."

Jay had talked Frankie, his fiancé, into a short engagement. I'd worried that he'd rushed into their relationship, but listening to him brag constantly about his woman had me wishing the fucking wedding was tomorrow – anything to shut him up.

"No women talk," I grunted out. "Not tonight."

"That's because someone doesn't want to talk about his ex," Jay teased, waggling a finger in my direction.

"How did you—Frankie."

Jay laughed, spreading his arms out wide, the minifig Lego tattoos on his right arm jumped with the movement. "You marry one, you marry them all."

"Don't I know it," I muttered, immediately pissed at myself when their three heads whipped around to stare.

"But you weren't married," Ren said.

"I'm not doing this." I stalked toward the locker room, ignoring their rapid-fire questions.

"Engaged? No. Maybe? Would he have broken up with her if they were engaged?" Jay asked, trailing behind me.

"I never saw a ring. But then I'd been doped up on prescription painkillers for about six months before they broke up."

"I can't remember Mai saying anything at the time. Only after they separated."

"Stop with the fucking gossip." I yanked my locker open, ripping my gym bag free to search for my towel.

"Pre-engaged?" Jay asked, his green eyes dancing as he shifted from foot-to-foot in front of me.

I paused in my search. "What the fuck is pre-engaged?"

"You know." He waved a hand around blithely. "You're committed and just waiting for the right moment to pop the question."

"Oh. Fuck," Ren muttered, catching the look on my face.

"We're not discussing Annie."

Theo dropped to the bench beside me, beginning to remove his prosthetic. "Linc made her an offer to become a partner in Garrett Paper. If the contract goes through, we'll be Garrett-Harris Paper by the end of the month."

Ren dropped his sweatshirt in his bag, whistling long and low. "Sheeeeit. That's massive."

"Does this mean you got the funding?" Jay asked, tossing a sneaker into his locker.

"With Annie's contribution we'll be solvent for another twelve months—longer if we can secure her a few more buyers."

"Which she's already done," I muttered, heading for the showers. "Unlike us, she actually knows how to run a successful company."

"Is he okay?" I heard Jay ask as I stepped into one of the stalls.

"No. He's been on edge since she accepted his offer."

I twisted the tap, grateful that the falling water blocked their conversation. I stripped off and stepped under the spray, wishing I could wash away the lingering doubts about this deal as easily as I did the sweat on my skin.

I wasn't the kind of guy to carry around regrets. When I made a decision, I stuck by it. Breaking up with Annie was the exception to that rule.

For years, I'd basked in her glow, simultaneously living for each one of her smiles while taking them for granted. I should have dedicated a lifetime to cataloging each one, instead here I stood. Fucking miserable that I didn't have a place in her life.

I closed my eyes, remembering her welcoming smile for that split second at the trade show. It'd felt like walking into the fucking sun after years of living in a cave.

"Fuck." I slapped a hand against the tile then did it again and again, anger boiling in my gut. "Fuck, fuck, fuck!"

"You okay in there?" Jay's voice floated over the shower partition.

I cleared my throat, switching off the water. "Fine. Just pissed we have to buy those dicks beer. I'm pretty sure they cheated."

"Those dicks?" Ren called. "I think you mean the champions of basketball. Theo and I are veritable Gods of the court."

"Blessed," my brother agreed. "No mere mortals can stand against us."

The bullshit flew thick and fast between the three of them as I dried off.

"You're all full of crap," I called, pulling on a clean shirt. "Let's get to the bar."

My cell beeped as I grabbed my keys.

Scott: Congratulations, the contract looks great. Subject to the fourteen day cooling off period, you're now Garrett-Harris Paper.

I stared at the message reading and re-reading the words, hardly able to believe it.

"Fuck," Theo barked from across the room, staring at his own phone. "It's done. It's actually, fucking done."

Our gazes clashed, my brother leaning heavily on his crutch as he balanced on one leg.

"I'd run across the room and embrace you but—" He grinned, gesturing at his missing limb. "Get your ass over here."

I bounded across, wrapping him in a back-slapping hug. "Fuck, we did it."

"Well," Theo corrected, pulling back. "Annie did it. But we'll take the credit."

I laughed, shaking my head. "Put your leg on. I wanna go celebrate."

Theo plopped down on the bench, reaching for his prosthetic. "Would you say you want to get legless drunk? Cause I'm already half-way there."

I groaned.

"Honestly, if we didn't look similar, I'd assume we were adopted."

"You wish buddy."

CHAPTER TWELVE

Annie

FRANKIE HELD UP HER SHOT, her cheeks flushed. "To Garrett-Harris Paper!"

I laughed, clinking my glass with hers. "I'll drink to that."

We downed our shots, both of us gasping as the tequila hit our tongues.

The fourteen day cooling off period had ended at 5:00pm that afternoon. A text from my lawyer had confirmed it—I now co-owned a paper company.

"And to my husband-to-be's cock. Thick, delicious, and ready to go." Frankie lifted the bottle, pouring another round.

The bride-to-be wore a wide sash, a crooked crown, a pink wheelchair, and a smile a mile wide. She looked like a woman who wanted to be married.

"You know I'll always drink to good D," I said,

catching her hand. "But how about we wait for Mai and Flo to arrive?"

She waved her hand dismissively. "Psh, they can catch up."

"Babe, they're lightweights. Do we really think they're gonna catch up? And Ren will kill us if we puke in his car. You know how he is with that dumpster fire of a vehicle."

Ren had promised to drive us home since the other men in our lives were busy with work.

She laughed, wheeling back from our table. "Alright, fair call. Let me go get some water and order some food and—"

I tutted, shaking my head. "As maid-of-honor it is my duty to wait on you hand and foot." I performed a small flourishing bow. "Allow me."

"Well, if you insist." She pulled her cell from her pocket. "I might spend this time sending some sexy texts to my fiancé."

Jay had left that morning to help a friend with a remote cabin build. Rather than travel the four-plus hours back and forth, he'd decided to camp at the build site. Less than twelve-hours since they'd last seen each other, Jay had already blown-up Frankie's phone with sexy requests.

I really love him for her.

I sent her a wink. "I expect nothing less."

I left her bent over her phone, a cute smile on her face. At the bar, I perused the menu, searching for the most carb-dense items available to fill our stomach.

"What the hell is a fry fritter?" I muttered aloud, flicking through the sticky pages.

"Three servings of already cooked fries dunked in batter and thrown into a fryer."

My head snapped up to find Linc standing beside me, his body casually leaning against the bar.

"Fuck. Where did you come from?"

An easy grin pulled at one corner of his mouth. "If we're talking in terms of existence then it depends on the belief structure to which you subscribe. Personally, I'm pro-Big Bang which means once upon a time monkeys—"

I rolled my eyes, tossing the menu on the counter. "You're an idiot." I leaned against the wood bar, trying to flag one of the bartenders.

"Mm," Linc hummed, stroking a hand over his short scruff. "And yet you've agreed to partner with me."

I glanced up, finding his dark gaze locked on me. I purposefully turned back to the bar, avoiding his look.

I forced levity into my voice, determined to brave this out. "Maybe I just wanted my name on a building."

"Shit Happens wasn't enough?"

"It's no Harris Industries. Or, in this case, Garrett-Harris Paper." Pleasure sparked in my belly, my lips curving into a self-satisfied smile.

"Ah, I see."

I cocked an eyebrow.

He grinned, slowly spreading his arms wide. "You just couldn't resist tying yourself to me."

A bitter taste filled my mouth, souring my mood.

"If I'd wanted that, we both know it could have happened."

The words landed between us with all the grace of a hippo performing a belly flop—drenching us both in unwanted memories.

Linc's arms dropped to his side, a strange expression crossing his face.

"Annie—"

"What can I get you?"

I turned to the bartender, pasting a bright smile on my lips. "I'll have three orders of the nachos, one of loaded fries, four orders of the house cider, and another pitcher of water for table four, thanks."

I could feel Linc's gaze on me as the woman rang up my order.

I tucked my card back into my purse, pausing when I saw Linc's expression.

"Why are you looking at me like that?"

"When we broke up...." He shook his head slowly. "It was for the best, Annie. Your reaction, and mine, proved we weren't ready for a relationship."

"It's nice you think that."

I pushed away from the bar, heading blindly for the safety of my friends.

"Annie, wait. Let me explain."

I spun, stepping forward to stab a finger into his chest.

"No," I whispered furiously, desperate not to cause a scene. "You can't make those kinds of jokes. You lost—" I broke off, sucking in a deep breath. "We have chemistry. That's undeniable. Would I let you fuck me?" I gave a one shouldered shrug. "Sure. But don't pretend we have something more than we do."

He stared at me, his expression inscrutable.

"Have a nice night, Linc."

"Annie."

I ignored him, turning on my heel to push through the crowd and get back to Frankie.

"Wait. Annie."

I slid into my seat, deliberately keeping my back to Linc.

"Not to be that friend—"

I snorted at Frankie's statement.

"—but that didn't look like a very polite conversation."

I poured myself a shot, lifting the tequila to my lips and downing it in one quick gulp. I slapped the empty glass on the table, stubbornly avoiding her knowing blue gaze.

"Don't look at me like that Frankie."

She held up her hands in a 'who me?' gesture. "I'm just making an observation."

I shot her a half-hearted glare. "I know Mai and Flo told you about our conversation."

"And I'm still pissed I missed it."

I flicked her crown. "This is your night, babe. I'm not ruining it with bullshit from my past."

"Even if that bullshit is a sexy six-foot-something-hunk-of-man-meat-glaring-at-you-in-a-way-that's-making-a-soon-to-be-married-woman-hot?" She fanned herself sending tendrils of her pink hair floating around her face.

I smothered a grin. "Even then."

She slumped in her wheelchair. "Damn."

I poured us another shot. "Shall we get white-girl wasted like that time in college when you—"

"We're here!" Mai guided Flo through the bustling crowd, one arm waving frantically over her head. "Sorry we're late. I wanted to—"

"Lincoln's here," Frankie interrupted, handing Mai a shot glass. "Flo, shot?"

"With a side of gossip? Yes please!" She leaned her white cane against the side of the table, her hand searching for the chair. "Is he looking at her?"

"You know I'm right here," I muttered darkly.

"I know, and I do not care for your participation in this conversation." Flo tilted her head to one side. "So is he?"

"He is."

"You're all the worst," I burst out, trying to ignore the strange emotions Frankie's confirmation had stirred in me. "This is Frankie's night and you're giving me shit? Worst fucking friends ever."

"Your potty mouthed protest is noted," Mai said, raising her shot to her lips. "But ignored."

"I don't mind." Frankie laughed, tipping her own shot toward me. "If it gets you out of your dating funk then I'm all here for it."

"Seriously," I muttered, pouring another round. "I hate you all."

Flo's hand found my arm, giving me a little squeeze. "We love you and you know it."

I grunted.

"And it's because we love you that we care. And because we care, we want you to be able to move past this. What happened to being friends with him?"

I pressed my lips together.

"Annie?"

"Maybe some people aren't meant to be friends."

Flo shook her head. "And maybe you have unresolved feelings that require deeper interrogation and forgiveness."

"Well fuck." Frankie slapped a hand on the table. "Am I the qualified psychologist or is that you? Because that is spot on."

"I've been listening to Esther Perel. Her podcast is—" Flo made a chef's kiss motion.

"Maybe we should nominate Annie and Linc. All that pent up rage. All the unresolved feelings. All the delicious sexual tension...." Mai let out a breathy moan as she shuddered. "The sex would be brilliant."

"Alright, enough. Seriously, this is Frankie's night. Let's celebrate her."

Flo raised her water glass. "To Frankie!"

"To Frankie!"

We clinked and drank, the tension easing from my muscles as we focused on our bride-to-be.

Our food arrived, the bar growing crowded as we drank, ate, and gossiped, celebrating Frankie's impending nuptials.

I'd blame the alcohol hitting my blood stream, but as the music changed, and the night wore on, my gaze began to wander, searching through the mass of bodies to find the one person with the power to wreck me.

There he is.

Across the room Linc stood, a beer in one hand, a pool cue in the other. Our gazes met, held. Anger from our argument still sizzled through my veins.

Why does he have to look so fucking good?

From his slightly too long hair, to his scuffed boots, he radiated effortless masculinity. His shirt stretched across broad shoulders, his jeans perfectly cupping a glorious ass.

I hate you.

The words had lost their heat. In addition to the arousal setting my skin on fire, his contract terms had made me question everything I thought I knew about him. So much of his proposal had focused on ensuring his employees were looked after—with next to nothing taken for himself. I hated that I now respected him.

I dislike you.

Back in the day make-up sex had been our default. I'd fabricated shitty arguments just to have him claim me. Our relationship had conditioned me to expect his touch, my body now aching and wanting after our confrontation.

I hate that I can't hate you. I hate what you're doing to me.

My stolen glances became longer, bolder, hotter. His expression said he wanted to fuck me, and the longer I stayed in the bar, the more I wanted to give in.

Flo's words intersected with Mai's, the truth of them swirling through in my tipsy brain, a dark ache pulsing between my legs.

Fuck.

Our gazes locked. I lifted my drink to my lips, downing the remaining cider.

"I'll be right back," I told the table.

"You okay?" Mai frowned. "You're flushed."

I pressed fingers to my warm cheeks. "I'm going to step outside for a few minutes. It's a tad hot in here."

"You need company?"

I waved them off. "No, no. Stay, I'll be back in a moment."

I turned, pausing to stare at Linc.

Am I really doing this?

I inclined my head toward the door, giving him a look I knew he'd recognize.

His eyebrows lifted, his body stiffening.

And there it is.

I despised that I still loved him. I hated that I still wanted him. It tore me apart that he had the power to make me feel things I didn't want to. Ten fucking years had passed between us but the pull of him hadn't diminished.

I wove my way through the crowd, heading for the exit, liquid heat warming my body.

The autumn air hit me, cooling my heated skin. I wrapped my arms around myself, moving down the crowded walk to lean against the side of the brick building.

Anticipation churned, the hairs on my body standing on end as I waited to see if he'd follow.

Your move, Lincoln.

The door to the bar opened, a drunk couple stumbling out, laughing as they staggered down the road toward Main Street.

I waited, my heart loud in my chest, my breath catching at every swing of the bar door. I ached for his touch, a desperate tension building inside me.

He's not coming.

Time beat slowly, realization dawning.

"Damn." I closed my eyes, my head dropping back to the cold brick. "Fuck."

"Fuck?" A familiar voice asked. "I can do that."

My eyelids flew open as Lincoln's hands settled on my waist, he bent slightly, his forehead pressing against mine.

"You're late."

"Does it matter?" One of his big hands glided down my body, moving to cup me.

I groaned, my hips shifting to rock against his palm, desperate for friction.

"I know what you want, Annie. Let me make you feel good."

"Here?" I asked, glancing back at the bar entrance.

"Come with me." He caught my hand, tugging me along. I followed blindly, surprised when he led me to a familiar old pickup.

"You kept her?" I asked, running my fingers along the side of the old truck.

"Of course."

He pulled the door open, holding it for me. "Your choice, babe."

I shivered at the need in his voice. "What are we going to do?"

His gaze dropped to my lips. "Make you come."

CHAPTER THIRTEEN

Linc

SHE WATCHED me with big eyes, the golden highlights catching in the dim light of the parking lot.

Get in the truck.

I held the door, waiting for her to make a decision.

I'd watched her all night, noting her alcohol intake, knowing she wasn't even close to drunk.

This had to be her choice. If I influenced her, it would give her a reason to deny what happened between us. But fuck if my palms didn't itch to pick her up and throw her in the cab.

"Make me come?" she asked, one hand pressing to her hip, a smirk touching her full lips. "That's a bold assumption."

Fuck I loved her sass.

I cocked an eyebrow, silently daring her to disagree.

"Fuck it." She placed her hand on the door, boosting herself up. "Do me."

I followed, slamming the door close behind me, watching her slide to the other side of the bench seat.

"Whatcha waiting for?" Annie asked, spreading her thighs. "Come taste."

"Fuck."

I ignored her invitation, determined to take my time. My hand wrapped around her ankle, lifting one leg.

I pressed a kiss to her calf, my first taste of her skin in ten years.

I missed you.

"What are you doing?"

The fabric of her skirt floated down her legs to pool at her thighs, her hands fisting the material.

"Savoring you."

She smelled like autumn, like a combination of crisp air, cinnamon, and pumpkin spice—her perfume bringing back a flood of memories.

She wore different scents for each season.

I wondered if I'd have noticed that back when we were together. If we'd stayed together, would I have appreciated the change in her skin, the fine lines and new bumps that now marked her as a woman? Would I have noticed the change in her golden eyes? The sweep of her hair as it cascaded across her breasts?

Or perhaps the better question was—would I have cared?

I removed her wedge, tossing it on the floor of my pickup, moving to do the same with her other foot.

"We don't need to get naked to have sex," she whispered.

"We're not having sex." I dropped her second wedge on the floor, my hands beginning a slow slide up her legs.

"No? Could have fooled me."

"Nope." My hands slipped under her skirt, grazing her inner thighs. "I'm gonna make you come then take you back to your friends."

She blinked.

"But—"

I swore, cutting her off. "Where the fuck is your underwear?"

My fingers tangled in her damp curls, her desire coating my hand.

"At home." Her head fell back, her body arching until her hips pressed up, welcoming me.

"I should spank you for this."

She shuddered, bucking a little against me.

That's new.

I leaned in, one hand cupping her pussy.

"Have you been a naughty girl?"

Her eyelids fluttered open, a moan slipping from between her sweet lips.

I rocked back to wrap one hand around her throat. "Look at me."

Annie's gaze locked with mine, her throat moving under my hand.

"Last chance. Say no and I'm out of here. Say yes and this—" I brushed a finger against her clit. "Is just the start."

I withdrew my hands, waiting for her decision.

"Linc?"

"Mm?"

She fisted my shirt, tugging me down. "Finger me."

Her lips caught mine.

Fuck.

I fucked her mouth, my teeth nipping at her greedy lips, drawing gasps and moans. I took advantage of her surprise, my tongue sliding inside her mouth, committing her flavor to memory.

Fuck. Fuck. Fuck.

I ached to mark her, to give her some visible sign of our time together—something that would force her to confront our connection and remember me every time she looked in the mirror.

I wrapped a hand around her neck, using my thumb to turn her head away from me.

"What—oh God."

My teeth gently grazed her earlobe, teasing her hot spots.

"Why does this feel so good?" she asked, her body arching under mine.

"Because it's us."

She tried to dismiss it but I caught her mouth with another punishing kiss, silencing her protest.

I ran my free hand down her body, determined that the next time we did this we'd both be naked. With an impatient tug, I jerked her skirt up, the material bunching in the tiny space between us.

My mouth continued to fuck hers as I worked a hand between us, my blunt fingers stroking the sensitive skin of her thigh, then up to her labia, teasing at her slit, her desire coating my hand.

Well, fuck.

She rocked against me, desperate little pleas for more whispered against my lips, her hips flexing in challenge.

I tightened the hand around her throat, keeping her still as my thick fingers parted her, stroking.

I knew what she liked. But now, I paid attention to her micromovements, to the catches in her breath, the pressure of her kiss, the sweet clutch of her hands as her nails dug into me.

I didn't want to just do what she liked—I wanted her to fucking love it.

"More," she begged, her tongue licking my lips. "More."

I built her up, slipping first one then another finger into her, my thumb rolling across her clit. I fucked her with my hand, memorizing every desperate gasp and harsh demand I ripped from her throat as I guided her into a lusty, delicious climax.

Her body arched, mouth ripping free as she came, the beauty of her searing into my memory.

"Fuck," I muttered, leaning down to nip her neck. "You're fucking gorgeous."

"You fucker," she groaned, collapsing back against the seat. "Fuck you. Seriously."

"Not tonight." I pulled back, moving us until my face was in line with her abdomen. "First, I'm gonna reacquaint myself with your sweet pussy."

"Sweet baby—" Annie groaned, her hands dropping to bunch in my hair as I brushed dragging kisses down her abdomen to the juncture of her thighs. I gripped her legs, a grunt of pleasure escaping as I held her open to tease her sweet cunt.

"Fuck, I missed you."

Her taste exploded on my tongue, rich and smooth—like the best whisky, it went straight to my head, my dick aching to feel her clutching around me.

Her legs flinched in my hands, her fingers tugging my hair this way and that as I devoured her.

"This was a terrible idea," she groaned, pressing herself more firmly against my mouth.

"Really? Seems like you're loving it."

She cursed, bucking. "Shut up and make me come."

My hand closed around her throat, my pressure gentle as I waited for her golden eyes to lock with mine.

"That's one," I told her, my thumb grazing the soft skin of her neck. "Do it again and I will turn you over and spank your ass until it's red."

She shuddered, her cheeks flushing.

I filed her reaction away for further examination.

"Or this?"

"Yes, that!" She thrust her body up, chasing my hand.

I returned to her clit. Teasing and circling, pressing and rubbing, determined to pull those greedy fucking noises from her.

"Come for me," I demanded, doubling my efforts. "Let me hear you break."

She shattered, her throat vibrating under my hand with a long moan as she came, her thighs shuddering, her body arching.

I rocked back on the seat, tracing small designs on her skin, loathed to let her escape.

Patience. Slow and steady. You need to rebuild trust.

"Wow," she muttered, her arm draped over her eyes. "I wasn't expecting that."

"What were you expecting?"

She lifted her arm, opening one eye to peek at me. "A half-hearted diddle with some sloppy kissing?"

I snorted. "Half-hearted? Annie, I'm harder than a fucking rock."

She closed her eyes, lazily stretching. "Mm, I could feel you. It's nice to see all of you has grown."

I leaned down, nipping at her lips. "Minx. Stop sassing me."

"I should go," she whispered against my lips. "They'll be worried about me."

I pulled back, moving to give her space. "You gonna tell them about this?"

She snorted, her grin wide and so stunningly gorgeous I couldn't help but trace the curve with my thumb.

She laughed, batting my fingers away. "You smell like me. Stop it."

I dropped my hand, watching her straighten her clothing and smooth her wild hair.

"You look different."

She froze. "Different how?"

I shrugged. "You're still the same Annie—full of fire. But you're...." I found myself at a loss to describe what I saw.

She reached for the door handle, her fingers clutching the lever. "Fat? Older? More jaded?"

"Who you were always meant to become."

She stared at me for a beat, eyes wide. Emotions

swam in their depth, but I couldn't for the life of me make out what they were.

"Good night, Lincoln." She shoved the door open, hopping from the cab. "I'll see you at work on Monday."

I watched her walk across the lot, everything demanding I follow her.

She paused at the corner, glancing back at the cab, her face illuminated by a street lamp. Even from this distance I could read her uncertainty and fear.

My hands gripped the steering wheel, needing something to hold on to.

She glanced back once more before disappearing into the bar.

"Fuck," I muttered, pinching the bridge of my nose. "Fuck."

Monday was going to be interesting.

CHAPTER FOURTEEN

Annie

At one time, Garrett Paper had employed nearly half the residents of Capricorn Cove. But two decades of cutbacks and downsizing, had reduced the workforce to a mere fraction of its hey-day, leaving three vacant buildings.

I placed my hands on my hips, surveying the giant warehouses, storage sheds, and vehicles I now officially co-owned.

Deal of the century.

The entire facility had a sheen of neglect to it—from the cracked paint and peeling letters on each of the buildings, to the rusted roofs and overgrown ivy climbing the sides of the buildings.

"We're going to bring you back to life," I promised, determined to make it happen. "Don't you worry."

"You know, talking to yourself is the first sign of insanity."

I turned, grinning at Theo as he walked up the long path, his breath misting in the cool autumn air.

"That's an offensive stereotype. You should stop saying it."

He paused, his head tilting to one side. "Is it? Fuck. You're right." He slung an arm around my shoulders, giving me a squeeze. "See? Already adding value to the company. Welcome aboard, partner."

My stomach flip-flopped with nerves. "I have to admit, I expected more of a fight from you guys regarding the name change."

We fell into step, heading for the main office building.

"You've seen the books—the financials say it all. We were in a bind and you bailed us out. The bigger surprise is that this was all Linc's idea. You know him, he's all about certainty and stability. That boy hates change and this is massive."

I paused, my steps faltering. "He does?"

Theo stopped, shoving hands into his pockets. "You don't think so?"

I shrugged. "I guess I only knew the old Linc, I don't remember him being particularly focused on stability."

Theo snorted, moving up the path. "Then you didn't know him as well as you think you did. My brother doesn't do change well."

I tried to conjure memories of Linc that belied Theo's statement, but hit a blank.

"Annie? You coming?" Theo held the door open.

"Of course." I shoved thoughts of the past away, determined to focus on the now.

The office building needed a full renovation. Samples of dusty, faded product lined grungy white walls, the linoleum floor under my feet peeling and marked from decades of use. The fluorescent lights flickered, lending everything a slightly agitated feel, the entire effect unwelcoming and off-putting.

"When was the last time this place had a good clean?" I fingered one of the sun-bleached posters, the advertising declaring a sale in 1973.

Theo snorted. "Maybe when Gramps still worked the place. Dad isn't exactly known as the kind to care."

I nodded, making a mental note to add renovations and cleaning to my to-do list.

Buying into Garrett Paper hadn't completely wiped out S#!T Happens savings, but it had put a giant hole in it. Looking around the shabby office building, I knew we'd need to invest more capital to get it in shape.

"Do you always leave the lights on?"

Theo shook his head. "I can almost guarantee Linc's already here. He's normally in around three."

"A.M.?"

Theo nodded, the light in his eyes dimming. "It's been a rough few months. Me? I'd be happy to see the back of this place. But Linc? He's fighting tooth and nail to keep us afloat. He wants to ensure our employees have financial security."

A weird fluttering sensation took up residence in my chest. "He cares."

"Cares?" Theo snorted. "This place is his life, not that he'd admit it."

I followed Theo down a short corridor to the main

office, my heart performing a weird tap dance in my chest.

I'd spent most of the weekend nursing what I'd called a hangover—though, if I were honest, it was more like heart-over. I hadn't been the slightest bit drunk when I'd agreed to get into Linc's truck. Horny? Yes. Drunk? No.

Which sucked, because I wanted to deny it had happened—or at least give myself an excuse. But every time I saw the hickey he'd left on my neck, I was left with only one truth—I still wanted him.

And that scared the shit out of me.

"Brother, look who I found skulking around outside." Theo shoved me through the office door and into—

"Wow." I stared around the room. "This isn't... wow."

This was not the same office in which I'd negotiated our merger. In the short weeks since we'd last met here, the ceiling had been painted black, the walls a crisp but warm white—except for one. The wall behind Lincoln's desk was navy blue and covered in white-framed black and white prints of the factory and employees. The desks had also been replaced, along with new ergonomic chairs, and updated monitors and keyboards.

My perusal complete, I finally turned my gaze to Lincoln. He watched me, one eyebrow raised slightly as if asking if this was okay.

"It's gorgeous," I told him, genuinely impressed by the newly remodeled space.

"We tried to make it welcoming. We'll eventually get to the rest of the building as well. Coffee?"

Had he painted it just for me?

I glanced at the coffee machine on the sideboard, my eyebrows raising. "We can afford an espresso machine?"

He snorted. "Fuck no. I bought this one out of my own pocket. We might as well get use out of it all day since we're here." He cleared his throat. "And your director said you need coffee to function."

Oh.

"That's thoughtful." I busied myself with my backpack. "And sure, I'd love one."

Who was this man? And why did he affect me so?

I pulled myself together, glancing between the three desks in the room. "Where can I set up?"

Lincoln pointed to the one in the middle of the U-shaped set-up. "We've nominated that as yours, if you want it?"

"Works for me." I dropped my bag on the desk and began to rummage through it. "Is there somewhere my team can work from? I'd ideally like to begin transitioning them across from our existing offices in the next few months."

"I didn't realize you would want your team here."

I glanced up, finding Lincoln frowning.

"It makes sense to bring them here. Co-locating means I can channel the rent I'm currently paying back into the business, and if they need me, they don't have to travel forty-five minutes for a chat."

Linc and Theo exchanged a look.

"What?" I asked, annoyed at their glance.

"It's been a long time since this building saw any significant use." Theo shrugged. "We have the space but it's...."

"Gonna need work. It's pretty disgusting. This room, the staff room, and the training room we prioritized for renovations, but the whole place needs a makeover." Linc ran a hand through his hair. "You sure you know what you're getting into?"

There were stress lines around his eyes and a tick in his jaw.

"Lincoln?"

He braced, lifting his head.

"Calm down." I pulled my laptop from my backpack, laying it on the desk. "We're good. I knew this was going to be work when I signed the contract. You're not telling me anything I didn't expect."

The tension in his body didn't ease.

"I've done the estimates," he said, crossing his arms and leaning against the sideboard. "Earliest we could be operational—subject to recruitment and the new machinery arriving, not to mention all the approvals and testing—is mid-April next year."

I huffed out a laugh. "Just jumping straight in. Buy a girl dinner first, why don't ya?"

The men didn't laugh.

I quickly crunched the numbers in my head. "I think that should work. I'll have to talk to Charlie—my head of supply—but the two contracts I've just negotiated aren't expecting delivery until June next year. We have time to get all our ducks in a row."

"What about your existing buyers?"

I pulled out my coffee mug and a bunch of pens. "My old supplier might have fucked me over, but the douchebag failed to realize that he needs to meet all the existing orders for the final months of our contract." I grinned, feeling a little like the cat that caught the mouse. "I increased our order numbers—if he can deliver, which he has to, then we're good for 12 months. And that's factoring in a five-percent increase in sales."

The brothers stared at me.

"Well, fuck," Theo muttered. "Remind me not to get on your bad side."

"Can he meet that demand?"

I raised one shoulder in a half-shrug. "He has to. It's in the contract."

"And if he can't?"

"That's my favorite part." I rubbed my hands together, delighted by my forethought. "When I wrote the contract I was petrified of being screwed over so included a clause that he'd have to pay me the value of the order plus twenty-percent to cover damages. He agreed."

"You're a shark." Linc shook his head, his teeth flashing. "I should have fucking known."

I gave a little curtsy. "Thank you."

After what had occurred last Friday night, I'd not expected the easy back-and-forth between us, or the gentle teasing. I'd assumed he would push me away or make this weird—not welcome me without even a hint of reference to our intimate moment.

I didn't quite know whether to be pissed off or relieved.

My desk set up, I dusted my hands, turning to my new business partners.

"Should we do a tour? I'd like to catalogue exactly what I'm getting into. Sheena will be by later today, but I want to get a feel for the place before we start discussing changes."

"Changes?" Linc asked, frowning.

Theo chuckled, inching toward the door. "How about I do morning rounds today and you take Ms. Harris for the tour?"

"Wait, what if— damn." I stared at Theo's rapidly retreating back, annoyed he'd left me alone. "Your brother enjoys avoiding conflict."

"He's a child."

"He's two minutes younger than you."

"And yet there are decades of difference in maturity."

We grinned, our gazes catching and holding. A beat of silence followed, something passing between us.

"About Friday night," I began, searching for the words.

"Don't."

"Excuse me?"

"Don't deny it, Annie." He stepped closer. "It happened. And, if I had my way, it would happen again."

"But—"

My cell rang, interrupting us. "Crap, it's Sheena." I raised it to my ear. "Hello?"

"I just pulled up. What in the ever-loving bullshit is this place? Did you seriously buy this?"

Grateful for the excuse, I turned away from Linc. "You were supposed to arrive this afternoon."

"It's your first day as co-owner of a paper company, the hell I'm missing even one minute." I heard her trip and mutter something distinctly unsavory under her breath.

"Sheena?"

"I'm booking us in for tetanus boosters. This place is rust central."

"Sheena," I repeated, trying to sound more authoritative and less amused.

"I was all for you being a badass but this place looks about two steps from the grave. We should burn it down and—"

"Sheena!"

"What?"

"Have you had coffee?"

"At this hour? Where the hell would I get coffee from?"

I reached for my to-go cup. "Where are you?"

"Standing in a giant crater of a parking lot."

"And people think I'm the dramatic one. I'll meet you outside."

"Seriously, Annie, what have you purchased? Not a single inch of this place looks safe."

I glanced over at Linc.

"It might not look like much right now, but with hard work we'll get there."

I hung up, slipping my phone into my pocket. "Sheena's here. I'll just get her a cup of coffee and we can start the tour."

"Annie, before we go, there's something I need to say."

I stuck the cup under the head, pressing one of the buttons. I leaned against the sideboard, crossing my arms. "Shoot."

"It's about Friday night."

I tensed, my belly dropping. "It was a one and done thing."

"Was it?" He crowded my space, shifting closer. "'Cause I want you. And I think you want me too."

I pressed my lips together, holding my ground. "Even if I do, it's a terrible fucking idea."

"Why?"

I lifted a hand, circling it to encompass the room. "We're business partners for one. Then there's our past. Not to mention our familial friendship group. People will have expectations of us. They wouldn't believe us saying we're only doing it for the sex."

"What if we don't do it just for the sex?" His hand reached out to glide along my side.

"Dating? Fuck off. We're not dating."

"Why not?"

Anger boiled, frustration warring with an undercurrent of desire as I pushed him back with one firm hand. "Because you left me at the altar without even a fucking explanation."

I snatched Sheena's coffee, screwing the lid on. "You might have forgotten, but I never will."

"Annie, I can explain—"

"Explain this." I flicked him the bird, heading for the exit. "We're business partners, Lincoln. Get that into your thick fucking head."

I slammed the office door on his stupidly attractive face, stomping down the depressing hall to find Sheena.

"Stupid men."

CHAPTER FIFTEEN

Linc

TEN YEARS before

The house felt like a crypt, hushed voices and stunted conversations now the only sounds allowed within these walls.

The accident had nearly robbed me of my brother—nearly, but there he slept, silent and at peace thanks to the painkillers and sedatives surging through his system.

I stared down at his face, my heart pounding as I fingered the letter in my hand. I'd agonized over it, struggling with every word, questioning if he'd forgive me.

Theo,

I'm marrying Annie. I know, I know. You're pissed, but I can't wait. Your accident proves life is too fucking short, and I know she's the one for me.

Forgive me for leaving you. I'll be back once Annie and I are set up. It'll just be the three of us.

Linc.

"Lincoln? What are you doing?"

My mother stood in the doorway, her severe face disapproving.

"Nothing," I answered, keeping my voice low to avoid waking Theo. "Just checking on him."

Eleanor sniffed, her gaze focusing on something behind me. "What's that?"

Fuck.

I snatched the letter. "Nothing."

"It's obviously—"

We both froze as Theo stirred. His eyelids fluttered as he teetered on the cusp of awakening. After a beat, his breathing evened out, his forehead soothing.

I gestured at Eleanor to proceed me, tucking the letter into my back pocket. In the hall, I gently closed the door, pausing to take a bracing breath before turning to look at the woman who'd birthed me.

"You're hiding something." Her eyes narrowed on the duffle bag in my hand. "Where are you going?"

The lie fell easily. "I'm headed to Ren's for a few days. We're gonna work on his fitness ahead of his exam."

She stared and I could see the moment she sniffed through my bullshit. As a politician, she'd had decades of experience dealing with the best liars around.

"You're going to that girl."

My teeth clenched, my hands curling into fists. "Annie. Her name is Annie."

"Why do you insist on seeing her? I've asked you numerous times to—"

"We're not having this conversation." I brushed past her, heading for the door.

"I'm speaking, Lincoln."

"And I'm done." I stopped, twisting to look over my shoulder. "Seriously, Eleanor, I'm done living under your roof. I'm done listening to the shit spilling from your mouth, and I am more than done with your attempts to control my life. You pissed off, leaving Theo and I alone with him. How often did we see you? Maybe once a year if we were lucky? You know who attended our little league games? Not you. Not Dad. Gramps. That man raised us while you went off and showboated around Washington."

"Now listen here—"

"No." I shook my head, eighteen years of resentment spilling over. "You listen. The only reason Theo's in this house is because you want the press coverage. Hero mother to the rescue—it plays so fucking well with an election coming up."

Eleanor's dark eyes flashed, her straight brunette hair swaying in time with her movement as she stalked toward me, her heels clicking sharply on the wood flooring.

Years later, that's what I'd remember—the click of her heels right before she delivered the death blow.

"You think I don't know about the engagement ring?" Her smirk held a touch of mocking. "Her father works as a janitor, Lincoln. Her mother is a cleaner. You're the son of a Senator. Do you really think she's an appropriate choice?"

I glared at her, hating every drop of blood we shared. I turned on her. "Goodbye, mother."

"You can leave but know this, if you walk out that door your brother's medical bills won't be paid."

I froze, my hand on the door knob. "What the fuck?"

"You're eighteen. How do you think this wedding will play out in the media? They'll assume you knocked her up—and I am pro-abstinence. I'll lose the evangelical vote." She shook her head. "I can't allow you to bring that kind of media scrutiny."

"You'd fuck over your own sons?"

She shrugged. "I'll do what I have to. You'll get over her."

I dropped my hand, impotent rage boiling my blood. "I hate you."

"Are you staying?"

"You've given me no fucking choice."

"Give me your phone."

"What?" My hand went to my pocket.

"Give me your phone."

"Why?"

"You're going to Washington. I expect you to spend the summer supporting my campaign. And you won't be speaking to that girl."

"Or you stop looking after Theo?"

She inclined her head back toward Theo's room. "The choice is yours."

I sucked in a breath; my chest tight. There would be no winning.

"Why are you doing this?"

Her gaze hardened. "Because I can."

"I'll call Walter, he'll—"

"The man who caused your brother to lose his leg?" She issued a humorless laugh. "Yes, I'm sure he'll take wonderful care of your brother."

My fists clenched. "At least let me call her. Let me explain—"

She turned away, her heels clicking down the wall. "I've told you your options. Leave the phone on the side table, the car is waiting in the drive, it leaves in five minutes."

I stared at her retreating back, my heart hurting.

My choices were my brother or Annie. Either way, one of them would get hurt.

I pulled out my cell, typing out a text, praying she'd understand.

Linc: I'm sorry, Annie, I'm not coming. I'll call you, I'll explain when I can. I love you. Trust me.

Annie

I waited on the courthouse stairs, a bouquet of cheap roses clutched in one hand.

"Where are you, Lincoln?"

A limo pulled up, a groom and his bride spilling out followed by their laughing, joyous bridal party.

The bride caught my eye as her groom led her up the stairs.

"Congratulations," she called, shooting me a big smile.

"And to you!" I watched, heart in my throat as they entered the building.

I couldn't wait to become Lincoln's wife. I couldn't wait to start our lives together.

My cell beeped and I unlocked the screen, reading the message.

Lincoln: I'm sorry, Annie, I'm not coming. I'll call you, I'll explain when I can. I love you. Trust me.

I stared at the text, reading and reading his words.

"Oh, God." I pressed a hand to my mouth, the roses tickling my cheek. "Theo. Something must have happened to Theo."

I pressed the call button, raising the phone to my ear, listening to it ring.

"You've reached Linc. Leave a message after the tone."

I hit end and tried again. And again. And again. Disbelief giving way to confusion then panic.

"Shit." I dialed his mother's number.

"This is Eleanor."

"Ms. Partridge? It's Annie Harris. Linc was meant to meet me for.... An appointment. I'm just checking that he's okay."

The phone line crackled, a long pause following my query.

"Annie, I'm sorry if he didn't tell you, but he's decided to support my campaign. He's moved to Washington for the summer. Lincoln left earlier this morning."

I choked, doubling over. "He's... gone?"

"Yes, dear. Didn't you know? We're very proud."

I couldn't find my voice.

"Was there anything else?" she asked, her tone light.

"No," I whispered, closing my eyes. "Thank you."

We hung up, reality finally setting in.

"He's not coming." My heart shattered, my legs giving

out. I collapsed on the stairs, the roses falling to the ground beside me.

"He's not coming." My voice broke, a sob heaving my body. "He's not coming."

By the time the happy couple left the courthouse, I'd pulled myself together enough to begin the long walk home, the discarded flowers all that remained of my failed elopement.

CHAPTER SIXTEEN

Annie

WORKING with Linc had to be its own form of torture. Observing him deal with clients and employees, watching him make decisions and include me in his thinking—it turned out I had a competency kink. I found men who had their shit together attractive.

It was the worst.

"I think that's everything," Sheena said, closing her laptop. "Are you staying for much longer?"

I nodded, absently rubbing at my stomach. "Mm, I wanted to get a head start on the pitch for our new sales next week."

She rolled her eyes. "You're a workaholic."

"Slide decks relax me."

"Sure, I believe you." She stood, stretching. "Don't stay too late. You've been working around the clock since the merger."

I glanced toward Linc's desk, finding him staring at

the monitor. A frown marring his brow, one hand absently stroking his chin.

"We've all been working hard."

"Just promise you'll try and go home before midnight."

I held up a hand. "I solemnly swear I will try to go home before midnight."

"Yeah, that sounded convincing." Sheena turned, waving at Linc. "See you next week, Boss Man."

He glanced up from his monitor, a smile replacing the frown. "Have a good weekend, Sheena. Thanks for your help this week."

I watched her leave, my stomach beginning to make whale noises.

I searched in my bag for one of my pills, washing it down with a gulp of tepid tea.

"Ugh." I made a face. "What time is it?"

"After five, why?"

I raised my mug. "That explains why this is cold. Where the hell does the time go?"

Linc and I had reduced our relationship to meaning-less banter interspersed with business-only conversations. In some ways, it felt like a relief to know we didn't have to force something deeper conversations and connection—in another, pure torture.

"Are you staying?" he asked, leaning back to stretch his arms over his head.

"For a little while. Why?"

He tapped his screen. "I think I found us a foreman."

"Really?" I scooted my chair back, heading for his

desk. "Let me see." Half-way to his desk my stomach lurched, a cramp overpowering me.

"Fuck." I bent, wrapping my arms around my middle.

"Annie? Are you alright?"

I'd known this was coming. The pains had been getting worse the last few weeks, coming more regularly and with greater intensity. I'd been living on borrowed energy, fueled by tea and coffee—not conducive to good health.

"Excuse me." Still hunched, I hurried out of the room, heading for the bathroom.

"Fuck, fuck, fuck," I whispered, trying to breathe through the pain.

I'd once heard that the screenwriter of the movie Alien had lived with Crohn's disease. When explaining the inspiration for the scene where the alien punches out of the guy's chest, he'd referenced his own journey with Crohn's.

I hated how fucking accurate it was. One minute you could be fine, the next it felt like a beast bubbling inside you trying to rip its way out. Sometimes I could feel it building, other times it blindsided me.

I pushed through the door of the bathroom, doing a quick shuffle into the first stall. With increasing urgency, I fumbled with my jeans, dropping to the toilet, doubling over as pain ripped through my body.

"I knew I should have called in sick," I groaned, losing control of my bodily functions.

"Annie?"

I heard a knock at the external bathroom door.

Please don't come in.

"Are you okay?"

"Fine," I lied, immediately undone by a cramp.

"I'm coming in."

"No! Go away." I dropped my head, embarrassment warring with pain. "I'm fine. I—" I gasped, panting as the cramps began to flow together. "I just need a minute."

"You looked grey when you ran out. Was it the chicken at lunch?"

I wish it was so easy.

"No," I said, trying to sound normal. "It's just—"

I hated moments like this, when I had to choose if I wanted to share my illness with someone or keep it hidden. I knew there was a privilege in invisible illnesses —they gave you the ability to pass as 'normal', hiding in plain sight. But they also sucked balls for the same reason. People often assumed you were fine, and when you were barely making it through the day, the words 'but you don't look sick' fucked with your mind, causing you to doubt your own illness.

A new cramp ripped through my body, stealing my breath.

"Fuck," I whispered, tears leaking from the corners of my eyes. "Linc?"

"Right here."

"I need you to help me get home."

The external door to the bathroom opened, his footsteps loud on the tiled floor as he came to a stop outside my stall door.

"What's happening?"

I closed my eyes, embarrassed by the sounds and smells my body was making.

You'd have thought after living with it for eight years I'd been normalized to a flare up. But introducing the reality of your illness to someone outside your sphere—it always felt scary. You became vulnerable, praying and hoping they wouldn't look at you differently.

"Crohn's disease, it's a pain in the ass. Can you just—" I groaned, pressing a hand against my stomach, desperately willing the pain to recede.

I heard him leave the toilet, my attention focused on breathing through the pain.

The door reopened, Linc's heavy footsteps echoing in the room.

"Annie, I have your things. Take your time, whatever you need. I'm right here."

I closed my eyes, beyond grateful he hadn't run screaming from the room.

"The antispasmodic should work soon." Another cramp kicked me in the gut, robbing me of breath.

"No rush, babe. I'm right here."

I closed my eyes, giving in to the pain, exhaling through the intensity.

I pulled a single square of toilet paper free from the dispenser, pressing it between my fingers.

Three-ply, the webbed series. 48 rolls to a pack.

I'd learned to play games with myself, disconnecting my mind from the pain in my body. Reciting facts about toilet paper, humming catchy pop songs, anything to take the focus away from the pain until the medication worked.

The intensity began to dim, the cramps easing.

"Do you have my bag?"

Linc slid it under the stall door.

"Thanks."

I cleaned myself up, patting a wet wipe over my sweating brow. Groaning, I forced myself to a stand, one hand pressed tight to my belly, the other braced against the stall partition.

"You okay in there?"

"Yeah," I breathed, forcing one exhausted foot in front of the other. I opened the door, looking up into his worried, brown eyes.

"Can you take me home?"

He wrapped an arm around me, supporting my weight.

"Absolutely."

CHAPTER SEVENTEEN

Linc

I UNLOCKED Annie's townhouse door then dashed back to the car, gently helping her from the passenger seat.

"Thanks," she whispered, still hunched. "I've got it from here."

"The fuck you do. You're grey and look like you're about to pass out." I wrapped an arm around her middle, guiding her to the door. "Let's get you inside."

She moved gingerly, her body shuffling as if she were glass and likely to shatter with the slightest bump.

Inside, I tossed her keys on her kitchen counter, looking around.

"Which way is the bedroom?"

"Second on the right."

I helped her down the hall, only letting her go when we reached her room. With a quick flick of my wrist I turned down her blankets, helping her crawl into bed.

"Thanks," she whispered, collapsing into a tight ball in the middle of the bed. "Sorry to ruin your night."

"You didn't ruin anything." I crouched beside her. "What do you need? How can I help?"

"My tote."

I headed back to the car, finding her bag stashed in the footwell. I locked up, then headed inside, typing out a text to Theo.

Linc: Annie's unwell. Just took her home, gonna stay and make sure she's okay. Give the guys my apology.

Theo: No apology necessary. Call if you need anything. Hope she feels better soon.

"Here." I placed the bag beside her on the bed, watching as she slowly rummaged through it to find a small blister pack.

"Do you need water?"

"Please."

I retrieved a glass from her kitchen, spotting a wheat bag on her counter. I snatched the thing, stuffing it in the microwave before heading back to the bedroom.

Annie had barely moved, her body curled in on itself, her arms wrapped tight around her middle as agonized sounds escaped from behind her tightly pressed lips.

"Fuck, Annie." I helped her sit up, holding the glass of water while she swallowed the pills, gently easing her back to the bed. I began to rub her back.

"Babe, I'm so sorry."

"I told you Crohn's is a pain in the ass," she whispered, her voice heavy with pain. "Ruins everything."

"Nothing's ruined. My plans were a hamburger with the guys, then Netflix."

She flinched, curling into a tight little ball.

"I'll be right back."

I retrieved the wheat bag, wrapping it in a cloth to bring back to her. Annie accepted it gratefully, pressing the warmth against her abdomen, her body still curled in on itself.

She fell silent, her concentration centered on the pain. In an agony of moments, Annie's body began to relax. Her hands loosened from around her stomach, the tension seeping from her shoulders.

I continued to rub her back slowly, watching for what felt like an eternity before the pain began to recede.

"Fuck," she whispered, her eyes closed. "I'm going to have to make a gastro appointment."

"Gastro?" I asked, my tone low and soothing.

"Gastroenterologist. My specialist. He monitors everything. I've been so good for so long. But multiples in one week is—" her voice broke, a stray tear sliding from under her scrunched-up eyelids. "It's not good."

Multiples? I hadn't noticed her like this, and the thought of her in pain without me knowing felt like a stab wound to the chest.

I brushed hair away from her cheek. "Do you know what causes it?"

She huffed out a laugh, her eyelids fluttering open, her gaze finding mine.

"Don't you think if I knew that I'd be avoiding it like the plague?"

I winced. "Stupid question.'"

"Yeah, but you're not the first to ask it. At least you didn't ask if I've tried turmeric powder or essential oils."

I attempted a joke. "Well, have you? I have a neighbor that sells lavender. I believe the FDA approved it for use. I've heard if you twirl it around your head three times on a full moon it'll cure anything."

She laughed then groaned, curling back in on herself.

"Sorry," I whispered, continuing to rub circles along her back. "I'm an idiot. It was a stupid question."

"It's okay. You'll do better next time."

I blew out a breath. "I hope so. Sometimes I feel like all I do is put my foot in my mouth around you."

She relaxed slightly, her head lifting, a shadow of a smile tugging at her lips. "Good thing I like acrobats."

"I hate that you nearly had to deal with this alone."

"Never alone," she murmured, her eyes drifting close. "My parents are here. And my friends. It's why I moved back to Capricor—" she groaned, doubling over. "Shit, move!"

I jumped back from the bed watching Annie stumble to the toilet, slamming the door shut behind her.

I pulled out my phone, searching for information on Crohn's disease.

Annie's groans grew louder, her pants beginning to sound like a wounded animal.

I fucking hated this for her, and I despised that I knew nothing about it.

She emerged from the toilet some time later, looking sweaty and flushed, wearing ragged and baggy sleepwear.

"You're still here."

I gently guided her back to the bed, handing her the freshly heated wheat bag.

"Get under the cover, baby girl. Let me take care of you."

She slumped into the bed, curling into a small ball, her gaze watching me as I moved around the room, turning off lights and plugging in her devices.

"Thank you."

I remained in the room until Annie's breathing evened out, her body slowly relaxing as the pills began to help.

My cell vibrated silently in my pocket. Determined not to wake her, on near-silent feet, I exited her room, gently shutting her door behind me.

My cell buzzed with another call.

Fuck.

I pulled it free, swiping a finger across the screen to check the notifications.

Walter.

I closed my eyes.

Fuck.

I lifted one hand to the back of my neck, squeezing as my other hit the call button.

"About fucking time," he grunted, picking up on the first ring.

I walked down the hall, putting distance between myself and Annie.

"What do you want, Walter?" I kept my voice low, determined not to wake her.

"You've fucked me over. A partnership? Who the fuck said you could do that?"

I moved to the far side of Annie's living area, looking into the dark of small patio area. "Theo and I did. You don't get a say any more. You're the one who fucked us up, remember?"

He made a sound. "Toilet paper. You've brought our name low."

"Toilet paper is going to save us."

"The fuck it is. You'll ruin my company."

My jaw clenched, a low hum buzzing in my ears. "Ruin the company? That's fucking rich coming from you. Where's the fucking money, Walter? Where's the hundreds of thousands of dollars you apparently invested?"

"You ungrateful piece of shit—"

I hung up, pacing the length of Annie's living space, trying like fuck to bring my emotions under control.

A picture caught my eye, the cluster of images on Annie's mantel halting my stride. I lifted it from the cluster, my finger running over her laughing, smiling face.

I took this.

She lay on a bed, laughing up at the camera. It'd been a happy moment between so many shit ones after Theo's accident.

I replaced the image, some of the tension easing from my shoulders.

She kept it.

The churning in my gut eased.

Feeling lighter than I had in months, I locked up her house, then stretched out on her sofa.

This time, I'm not going anywhere.

Annie

I woke to Linc placing a glass of water and some toast on my bedside table.

"Shit," he whispered, grimacing. "Sorry. Go back to sleep."

Yesterday's episode had wiped me out, and I lay under the blankets already anticipating a bed day.

I rubbed sleep from one of my eyes. "I didn't realize you stayed."

Linc lifted an eyebrow. "You were in pain, where else would I be?"

A curl of pleasure unfurled in my stomach.

I moved gingerly, noting the new aches and pains. "Thanks for the toast."

He sat on the edge of the bed. "Do you want eggs?"

I shook my head. "I don't have any."

"I went out. The Crohn's and Colitis group said eggs were good during flares." He reached down beside my bed, handing me a giant wheat bag. "And I got you this. Your other one is tiny."

I found myself at a loss for words. "I don't know how to take this. Why? You never cared before."

"I cared, Annie."

I sat up in the bed, moving to rest my back against the headboard, the plate of toast balanced on my knees. I watched him, chewing slowly.

"Tell me why you never showed up."

"Is now the right time to be having this conversation?"

"Is ever?"

"I just meant—" He gestured at my abdomen. "It feels

wrong to add emotional trauma when you're still in physical pain."

"Physical pain can never hurt as much as emotional. Physical pain you can take pills and potions, and learn to deal with." I laid a hand over my chest. "But the kind of festering wounds that sit in your heart and soul? Those cut the deepest. They're the ones with the ability to leave wounds that will never heal."

"You're far too wise."

I grinned, lifting my toast. "Speak, Lincoln. Let's pop the festering wound and allow it to heal."

He sighed. "Eleanor found out about our elopement."

My brows lifted. "Oh."

"And she threatened Theo."

"Threatened how?"

His hands curled into fists, his head dropping. "Said she'd stop paying his medical bills if I didn't move to Washington for the summer."

"Fuck." I winced. "That's low. Did she want you there for the election?"

I nodded. "The timeline was—quick. She laid it out then and I only had time to send you that one message." He ran a hand through his hair. "I should have done more. I guess I was in shock and just reacted. By the time I came to my senses, I was on a plane."

My stomach began to gurgle, a familiar precursor to more forthcoming unpleasantness.

This had been the most honest and open conversation we'd had about the break-up, and I was about to cut it short.

"Coulda, woulda, shoulda." I reached out, squeezing

his hand. "Life goes on. Would I have founded Shit Happens if you were around to buy toilet paper for me? Probably not. Would you have stayed in the Cove and become an awesome boss? Probably not."

A dull cramp rippled through my gut.

"We need to talk about this—all of it. I want to know more and talk it through but—"

"You're unwell and need rest."

"Yeah." I squeezed his hand. "Thank you for the toast. And for buying me eggs."

He shrugged, getting to his feet. "I should let you sleep. You'll call if you need anything?"

I nodded.

He pressed a kiss to my head. "Sleep well, Annie."

Despite the flare, I spent more time than I'd like analyzing that kiss.

CHAPTER EIGHTEEN

Annie

"Have you ever heard of coprophilia?" Frankie asked from her spot on the sofa.

I finished reading my sentence, marking my place with a finger as I reluctantly pulled my gaze from my book. "What?"

"Coprophilia," she repeated, her gaze locked on the tablet in her hands. "Have you heard of it?"

Mai and I exchanged a confused glance.

We were crashed out across Frankie's living room floor, books in hand. Mai seemed to be on a motorcycle club kick lately having read Nina Levine's Storm series from start to finish, while I had fallen into a delightful rom-com from Megan Wade involving a donut van, a police officer, and a hilarious plus-sized heroine.

Flo pulled an earphone free, shifting to sit up on the other end of the sofa. Ace lay beside her, snoozing on the floor.

"Did you say something?" she asked, tapping on one of the earphones to pause her audiobook.

"Frankie's asking if we've heard of coprophilia and interrupting what is a supremely awesome red and read night," Mai said dryly, holding her glass of Shiraz aloft.

"Is this an essential question?" Flo asked. "I was just getting to the good part."

"Which book is it?" I asked, reaching for the half-empty wine bottle.

"Bec McMaster's The Mech Who Loved Me. I need these two to fall in love right now."

I snorted, pouring each of them another glass. "You always need them to fall in love. When's the last time you read a crime thriller?"

"Never," Flo retorted cheerfully. "I love love, and no one can take that away from me."

Our book club consisted of quarterly meet ups where we came dressed in our favorite loungewear, chatted for a few hours, ate copious amounts of cheese washed down with red wine, and then read whatever book took our fancy.

Pity my new steroid medications had relegated me to drinking tea.

"Back to me." Frankie clicked her fingers at us impatiently. "Have you guys heard of it?"

We shook our heads.

"Damn." She sighed, slumping on the sofa. "I'm gonna have to look it up and Jay is going to freak."

"Why?" I asked, spreading some delicious double brie on a plain cracker. "What is it?"

"I got a listener letter—"

"Boo!"

We tossed pillows and napkins her way.

"I know! I'm sorry! I know work is off the table on R'n'R nights but I forgot to find a listener letter for next week's podcast episode so thought I'd quickly have a look and—"

"And?" Mai asked, taking a sip of her wine.

"And this person wants to know more about scat play."

I coughed, the cracker lodging in my throat.

"What the fuck?" Mai swore as Flo recoiled.

"This is something people actually do?"

"Mm," Frankie nodded thoughtfully. "And your reactions are extremely telling. What's the rule in this friendship group?"

"Babe," I said hoarsely, pounding my chest to try and clear the remains of cheese from my lungs. "You know we would never yuck someone's yum, but... poop? Even I— the Queen of the Porcelain Throne—wouldn't go that far."

"And hence why we're going to discuss it on the podcast."

I gagged a little. "I think I'll pass."

Frankie tilted her head to one side. "Actually, we might talk about all bodily fluids."

"I'm afraid to ask, but all?" Flo asked, clutching her glass.

"Scat, golden showers, blood play. Did you know—"

"Nope," I shook my head. "Absolutely not. You are not going into detail on this. Rope? Yes. Toys? Absofreakin'-lutely. Bodily fluids?" I shuddered. "No. Hard, *hard*, pass."

"I could never be a sexologist." Mai lifted her glass in toast to Frankie, taking a long gulp. "Too much weird stuff. I don't need to know this much information about people. People are weird and gross and I don't have time for that."

"Agreed. I'm also not sure how you discover it's your thing but I definitely just discovered it's not mine." Flo gave a delicate shudder.

"Well, that ruined my vibe." I tossed my Kindle on the coffee table. "Any other topics you want to discuss, Frankie? An armpit fetish maybe? Feet perhaps?"

She sniffed, tossing her pink hair. "If you were a true friend, you'd know I did a four-episode special last season on how to pleasure different parts of the body."

I snorted, settling back against the giant pillow I'd commandeered. "Of course you fucking did."

"Speaking of ruining vibes." Flo leaned in. "What's this I hear about you and Lincoln, Ms. Annie?"

I blinked. "What?"

"I heard he was seen leaving your house last week at a *very* unreasonable hour."

I stared at my friend, once again startled by her gossip sources.

"Wait, you sat on this for a week?" Mai huffed, crossing her arms. "You're a terrible friend."

"I thought you'd appreciate waiting for a time when we could grill her together."

Mai glanced at me, her expression sharkish. "You're

forgiven." She waggled a finger in my direction. "Now spill, Annie."

I blew out a breath. "Not much to say. I had a flare up at work, Linc took me home and stayed the night."

"He stayed?" Flo pressed a hand to her heart. "Oh, how—"

"Don't say it!" I scrubbed a hand over my face. "It's not like that. He slept on the sofa. We're—" I hesitated, unsure how to describe what we had.

"Friends? Lovers? Colleagues?"

"Friends-in-progress."

They laughed.

"I'm serious. We're not quite there, but we're also not-not there. Do you know what I mean?"

"Absolutely not. But I'm glad you think you do."

I rolled my eyes, annoyed that Flo wasn't giving me room to escape. "He's growing on me. But trust comes hard."

"Why *did* you break-up?" Frankie asked, propping her chin in her hand. "You've never told us."

The words hovered on the tip of my tongue, the truth aching to be set free.

I wanted to tell them. I truly did. But I feared their reactions. Ten years ago, it had been too shameful for me to admit. Now it felt like it was too big a secret to simply lay out.

Years of listening to self-help podcasts, and reading about self-love had taught me not to believe the lies I'd been feeding myself.

I sucked in a deep breath, holding for a beat before exhaling slowly, determined to finally let go of the hurt.

"He asked me to marry him. We were going to elope at the courthouse. He never showed up."

They gasped, three faces paling.

"How could you not have—"

"That jackass! I'll pickle his balls in—"

"Oh, Annie."

Flo held her arms open, and I moved, welcoming her comfort. She rocked me back and forth as the hurt came, tears flowing.

"There's a lot of unpack here." Frankie shuffled down the sofa to lay a hand on my back. "But the only question that really matters is, what do you need?"

I huffed out a wet laugh, grateful to have these women in my life. "Nothing."

"Look, it's nice that you two are all warm and fuzzy love, and concentrating on our wonderful woman here, but me?" Mai brandished a cheese knife threateningly. "I'm gonna hunt that motherfucker down and cut his balls from his—"

"Mai!" I laughed, wiping at the remainder of my tears. "You can't do that, you'll get arrested."

"I'll find a lawyer. A female who'll organize a jury full of scorned lovers. Not one of them will convict me."

I yanked her into our impromptu group hug. "I love you guys."

"And we love you." Frankie squeezed me tight. "I'm disappointed you haven't let me help you process this."

"I thought I had."

The bitches I called friends burst into laughter.

"Wow." I pulled back, making a face. "You guys really are the worst."

"But you love us." Flo ran a hand through my hair. "And we love you."

"Sometimes," I grumbled, leaning into her hand.

"All the time."

I made a non-committal sound.

"Have you two discussed it?"

"Not in any detail. He's begun to explain what happened but I was mid-flare and I couldn't process that bombshell despite really, *really* wanting to deal with it." I pressed a hand to my stomach. "She's a real dick."

"And then you took the week off to recover."

I nodded.

Chronic illnesses weren't things you could just set and forget. Living with an illness required major, ongoing maintenance. You had to feel your body out and understand its peaks and flows, listening carefully to what it needed.

I'd taken a week off to rest and recoup, leaving Sheena and Charlie to support Linc and Theo. Owning my business carried a shit ton of stress, but the ability to hand over my baby to the trusted team I'd built around me was a definite perk.

"So, you haven't seen him since he slept over?"

"That's the thing—I have. He's been by every day. He bought me eggs because he'd read that they're good to eat during a flare. And a new heat pack because he worried my other one wasn't big enough. He's doing all these tiny, thoughtful things and I...."

"You?" Frankie prompted.

"I kind of love it. And that is terrifying."

"Are you going to talk to him?" Flo asked, beginning to braid my hair.

I considered it, wondering for the millionth time if there was value in retreading old ground. I had yet to convince myself our conversation would be worth the inevitable heartache.

"I might." I blew out a breath. "Or I might not."

"Closure is important and it is possible to achieve without getting a full picture from the other person." Frankie squeezed my arm. "The bigger question is, do you trust him? You're business partners now, you can't have animosity or unresolved feelings lingering. It won't work in the long term."

"I really hate when you're right."

She brushed a stray hair from my cheek. "Honey, don't you know? I'm always right."

I gave her a little shove then sighed, my eyes closing. "'Trust is....'" I trailed off, struggling to find the words to articulate the complexity of emotions swirling in my gut. "My head, my heart, and my gut are fighting."

"Say more," Mai prompted.

"He chose his brother over our relationship. Yes, it was for the noblest of causes, but there's this lingering doubt—what if he does it again?" I dropped my head, my hair trailing through Flo's fingers. "I can't go through that. It'll wreck me."

"Trust is hard to recapture." Frankie lay a hand on my leg. "But I know you, Annie. If you didn't trust him at least a little, you'd have never agreed to this merger."

I filed that away to process later. "And then there's me."

"What about you?" Flo asked.

"I also played a part in this. He didn't operate alone. I'm dramatic by nature—" I grinned at their reactions. "I know, I know. Understatement of the year. I'm not going to change who I am. I like who I am. But who I am in a relationship with him isn't someone I want to be again."

"Because of the fighting?" Frankie's blue gaze had taken on a clinical look.

The benefits of being friends with a qualified sexologist.

I nodded. "I can see now that what we had wasn't mature. We loved each other—passionately, deeply. But we were kids. Would we have grown together? I like to think so, but I don't know. I don't want someone who'll revert me to who I was in high school. I want a life partner who'll build me up."

I swallowed, sharing the one secret still between us.

"I'm attracted to him. And the night of Frankie's bridal shower, I let him eat me out in the cab of his truck because I couldn't say no."

They exchanged glances.

"Did you enjoy it?"

I closed my eyes, a warm flush heating my cheeks. "Yes."

"I told you she'd been gone a while," Mai muttered, Flo shushing her.

"Where to from here?"

"God knows." I dropped my head into my hands. "I know I have to speak with him. We need to clear the air."

"When?" Flo prompted. "Make a decision."

"I don't know." I twisted to look at her over my shoulder. "When would you like me to, Ms. Romantic?"

"Tomorrow. You should go to his house with breakfast and get it all out in the open."

A flutter started in my chest.

"That's not a bad idea," Mai said slowly. "We could ambush him. He'll be sleepy. I'll bring rope and—"

Frankie threw a pillow at her head. "Enough with the threats of bodily harm. We love you but I'll add you to a watch list if you're not careful."

"No one can keep me down!" She leapt to her feet, holding the pillow above her head. "I am Mai, the Magnificent Militant Murderess! I'll defend your honor!"

After she'd pounded us with the pillow, I lay on the sofa, my head in Flo's lap while she braided my hair, considering her suggestion.

Breakfast. I could do that.

CHAPTER NINETEEN

Linc

I PAUSED MID-SIP, a pounding at my door interrupting my morning coffee.

"Who the hell visits at stupid-o-clock in the morning?"

I glanced through the peephole, my eyebrows rising.

"Annie?" I yanked the door open, staring at the woman hovering on my porch. "What are you doing here?"

"Can I come in?" She lifted the multiple casserole dishes and Tupperware containers in her hands. "I brought breakfast."

I stepped back, granting her entrance. "Do you need a hand?"

"No, I got it—oh, nice place." She paused in the entry, kicking off her shoes. "Where's the kitchen?"

"Uh, down the hall."

"Great." She bustled in, commenting on the furniture, my wall hangings, and the paint work.

Theo poked his head out of his bedroom, his hair disheveled. "Is there a girl in our house or am I still dreaming?"

"Annie's here. She brought breakfast."

He perked up. "Breakfast? As in food that didn't come from a cereal box?"

"I find it telling that your priority is breakfast and not Annie."

"Psh." He waved a hand my way. "Annie's awesome but we see her every day. Breakfast I didn't have to make?" He patted his stomach. "That's a unicorn moment."

I rolled my eyes, kicking the front door shut. "I pity your future partner."

"My future partner will understand my needs and ensure I am always well fed. Speaking of...." He shuffled out of his room, crutch tucked under one arm. "Let's eat."

"How about you put a shirt on first?"

"Can't. Food calls."

I growled, stalking after him.

"Whoa." Theo halted in the doorway, his head bobbing in approval. "Nice."

Annie had made herself at home. A selection of muffins were spread on a platter I'd forgotten we owned, waffles and donuts piled on plates, a fruit salad in a clear mixing bowl.

"Annie," my brother groaned, shuffling toward the feast. "Marry me."

She laughed, tossing her hair. "You'd be sick of me within the week."

"But oh, what a week. Imagine the breakfasts. The lunches. The dinners!" Theo groaned, sliding onto one of the bar stools. "I'm willing if you are."

"As wonderful as that offer is." Annie's gaze met mine, a vulnerable expression crossing her face. "I'll pass. Actually, Theo. I'm here to talk to Linc. Could you give us a minute?"

"And miss this?" he asked, snatching a muffin from the counter. "Fuck no. You two can leave. His room is free."

I glared daggers at my brother's back. "Theo, get out."

He ignored me, biting into a muffin, moaning around his mouthful. "It's still warm."

With a sigh, I inclined my head toward the hall. "My room's down here, if that's okay?"

Annie nodded. She leaned over to ruffle Theo's hair. "When the oven timer goes off, that means you can take the breakfast casserole out."

He perked up. "Bacon?"

"And eggs and a spicy bean mix that would put me in hospital for a week if I ate it."

He cackled, forking a waffle. "All the more for me."

She followed me down the hall and into my bedroom, her head tilting back as she surveyed the space.

"You didn't take the master?" she asked.

"The attached bathroom is accessible—made sense for Theo to use it."

She nodded, moving to my bed and sitting down. "You've got good taste."

I watched her run a hand over the rich grey coverlet.

I leaned back against the door, crossing my arms and hooking one ankle over another. "Are you feeling better?"

She lifted a hand to pat her cheeks. "Steroids always add about five pounds in immediate water weight, but gosh do they make me feel good. Except for, you know, the insomnia and slightly exhausting energy bursts."

"But you're getting better?"

She stared at me, something passing across her face. "Linc, Crohn's is a life-long illness. I might be able to achieve remission at some point, but even that comes with uncertainty. Better is relative. Am I as sick as I was? No. Am I sicker than I'd like to be? Yes."

I shook my head. "I did it again, didn't I?"

She nodded.

"Sorry."

"It's okay. You're learning. It's when you know better and still do it that I get pissed off."

I cocked my head. "That feels like a segue."

"Maybe." She sighed. "We should talk about the other night."

"You sure you're up for this?"

"No, but it needs to happen."

I took a seat beside her. "Ask me what you want to know."

She stared down at her hands, her fingers beating out a nervous tap. "Hating you has taken up an enormous amount of space in my life. It feels monumental that we could be at a healing point." She glanced up. "And yet I'm so fucking angry at you, Lincoln. There's all this rage inside me." Her hands curled into fists. "I'm hurt you chose to let me go through life believing the worst of you."

"I'm sorry."

"You know what I experienced the moment you left me on the courthouse stairs? Rejection. You know what I felt?" She turned, pounding a fist against her chest. "Shattered. Broken. Alone. Love doesn't leave someone on their wedding day. Love doesn't send them a text. And when you came back? All you did was avoid me."

My chest ached. "Tell me what you need from me."

She wrapped arms tight around herself once more. "Explain it to me. Explain what happened from the beginning."

"Eleanor." My mother's name tasted bitter on my tongue. "She blackmailed me."

"I just don't understand why didn't you tell me that in the text?"

"That fucking text." I closed my eyes. "Because I wasn't thinking. If I'd known that would be our breaking point, I'd have done everything differently."

Annie's hand found mine, squeezing gently. "Okay, I'll cut you some slack for the text—I mean your own mother doing something like that? If that's not the definition of a toxic relationship I don't know what is."

"How about Walter?" I joked.

She shuddered. "Are you guys in counselling? In the fucked-up parents' stake, you're up there."

"We were. Following Theo's accident, Gramps arranged it. We went and dealt with our issues."

Except for you.

"What happened after you got to Washington? Why didn't you call me there?"

I knew this was gonna hurt.

"When I got off the plane, I knew I needed to get back to you. I didn't have any money or clothes. It was stupid and irresponsible but I ran. I worked for cash under the table, walking and hitchhiking my way back to the Cove."

She swallowed. "Those four weeks of silence. It wasn't because you were ghosting me. It's because you couldn't."

I nodded.

"And then you came back and I refused to speak to you." She pressed a hand to her mouth, her breath catching. "Lincoln."

"I tried. But then Theo got that infection and ended up back in the ICU. And Gramps had his first heart attack and—" Fuck it hurt to admit. "I couldn't cope. I retreated, falling into survival mode."

We sat quietly, her fingers tracing the lines of my palm.

"The day," she said softly. "I knew for sure it was over wasn't at the courthouse."

"No?"

She shook her head, her fingers stilling. "It was when you pulled out of college. All those dreams we had—all the work we put into getting there, and you just threw it away."

"I used the money for Theo. To pay his medical bills."

Annie stared at me. "Your college fund?"

I nodded.

"Lincoln."

I closed my eyes. "I don't regret it, but don't tell him. He doesn't know."

She brushed a hand across my jaw. "Why not?"

The words stuck in my chest. "It's complicated."

We fell silent, our hands interlocked.

"I loved you, Annie." I brushed fingertips along her jaw. "If you take nothing else away from this conversation, know I loved you. You don't get over that kind of love." I chuckled. "I think our chemistry proves that."

"Then why didn't you try again when I moved back here?"

"I wanted more for you than a broke guy working for his grandfather. You had dreams. Who the fuck was I to take them away from you?"

She shook her head. "So you decided what was best for me without actually asking." She bumped her shoulder into mine. "Don't *ever* do that again."

I absorbed that blow. "I know. I'm an idiot."

Tears glistened on the ends of her eyelashes. "You're not. I think we can both agree we contributed our own set of mistakes to the relationship." She sighed heavily. "I hope you know you've made it really hard to hate you."

"I see my ploy is working." I sobered. "Forgive me?"

She leaned against me, resting her head on my shoulder. "I'm not saying I'll forgive you today—I still need time to process. But I'll try."

"Thank you."

She glanced up. "Will you try as well?"

I nodded.

We sat for a moment longer, an easy silence settling between us.

"Are you two fucking in there?" Theo called down the hall. "'Cause the casserole is ready and I *will* eat all of it if you don't stop me."

The tension broke, an easy truce settling between us.

I stood, holding a hand out to her help her up. "Breakfast?"

She stared at my fingers, a tiny battle waging behind her eyes. When she placed her hand in mine, it felt like a victory.

"Now that all the secrets are out, let's save your brother from himself."

I followed her into the kitchen, guilt tightening my chest. She thought every secret had been revealed, but one remained unspoken between us.

I still loved her.

CHAPTER TWENTY

Annie

I RAISED MY PHONE, snapping a selfie of me in a hard-hat, winking at the camera.

"When I signed up to be a director of your company, no one told me I'd be required to purchase a construction outfit."

I looked over my shoulder to find Sheena stomping through the empty warehouse toward me, Charlie hot on her heels.

"But isn't it lovely?" I asked, sighing dreamily. "Look at her. She's so pretty."

They fell in beside me, watching the workers begin the install of our newest purchase.

"What is it exactly?" Charlie asked, turning his head to the side. "Some kind of roller?"

"Better. It's a sorter."

"Huh?"

I pulled the plans out of my back pocket, unfolding the paper.

"This warehouse will be where we store, sort, and pulp." I pointed to the various machines and diagrams on the plan. "We're going to begin taking inventory of paper in January. Once here, it will be sorted into various types to allow us to work out what's usable. Then it'll be broken down." I ran my finger along the plans, showing where each step of the process started. "And cleaned, screened, de-inked, thickened, brightened, and dried. Once the pulp is ready, we'll add some additional fibers, if required, then the pulp will be pressed, and dried, and then we'll have our paper." I gave a happy little dance. "It's happening. It's actually happening!"

"As long as everything can fit inside it will."

I glanced over my shoulder sticking my tongue out at Linc. "Don't you dare rain on my parade."

"I'm not. Just being realistic."

"That," I said, pointing at him with squinted eyes. "Is rain. You're a thunder cloud coming right at me buddy. Turn around, this flower doesn't need any water today."

He rolled his eyes, stopping beside me to watch the installers. "Theo buzzed, said everything is on track."

I clapped him on the shoulder. "Now that is the kind of news I like to hear."

He reached into his back pocket to pull a post-it note free. "Your current supplier called." He handed me the message, a shadow of a smile touching his lips. "Nice guy. I can see why you wanted to stay with him."

I glanced at the note, a chuckle escaping. "Ah, I see he's heard about our recent merger."

"I paraphrased but the word 'motherfucker' was mentioned once or twice."

"That sounds about right." I tucked the note into my pocket, looking back at the sorter with a happy little sigh. "Do you ever think about how lucky we are?"

"Lucky?"

I gestured at the machine. "That this is our life. We're bosses, Linc. We get to decide what comes next for this business. The sorter is the beginning of that journey."

He stared at me for a beat then turned on his heel, stalking off.

"What did I say?"

Sheena shrugged. "Nothing offensive as far as I could tell. But then I'm not the man madly in love with you."

Charlie nodded. "She's got a point."

I rolled my eyes. "You're both terrible."

"Are you ready for the wedding tomorrow?" Charlie asked, holding up his tablet. "Is there anything you need us to finalize while you're on leave?"

I straightened my hardhat, mentally running through my to-do list.

"One of you needs to follow up with the Artist Guild to finalize the samples we asked for. I want to get them locked in so we can start promotion for our Halloween line."

"And Colton?" Sheena asked, a glint in her eyes.

"I'll deal with him shortly."

"Oh look," Charlie said, his voice dropping. "Lover boy returns. And with... craft activities?"

Linc walked toward us, his long strides eating up the

space, a paint can in one hand, brushes and spray in the other.

"What's this?" I asked.

"You're right, this is the start of the Garrett-Harris journey." He juggled the items in his hands, thrusting one of the brushes at me. "We need something to commemorate it."

My heart began to flutter wildly. "What are you thinking?"

He waggled the brush. "Take it and you'll see."

I ignored the delighted looks from Charlie and Sheena, and accepted the brush, following him across the warehouse to one of the corners of the massive building. Linc set the equipment down, using the spray to clean the dusty concrete floor, mopping it with a rag he pulled from his back pocket.

"You can go first."

I crouched beside him, watching as he popped the lid of the paint can. "Ah, I see. But what do I write?"

"Whatever you want." He grazed a hand along my cheek. "You're the boss."

My breath caught, our gazes holding.

"Linc."

He kept doing this, these small acts of kindness—hot coffee on my desk each morning, cute notes and funny texts. I'd found a Crohn's survival kit on my doorstep, featuring electrolytes, a hot water bottle, wet wipes, and a small tube of turmeric. Every time Linc made me smile it became harder and harder to remember why dating him seemed like a bad idea.

A throbbing ache began to pulse between my thighs. We leaned toward each other, swaying closer.

He's going to kiss me.

A loud, crunching, thump broke our connection. I fumbled, dropping the brush as our heads twisted to watch the installation.

"It's fine," one of the contractors called, shooting us a thumbs up. "Just settling into place."

I shuffled away from Linc, dipping my head to hide my flushed cheeks with my hair.

What am I doing? Kissing him would be a terrible idea. You already slipped up once. You can't allow it to happen again.

Giving myself a mental shake, I lifted the paint brush, coating it with a generous amount of navy paint to write on the concrete.

"Annie Harris, badass boss. When S#!T Happens we're here to help," Linc read aloud, grinning "I like it."

I handed him the wet brush. "Your turn."

He hunched over, his bold stroke in contrast to my swirled writing.

"May the company live long and prosper—Lincoln Garrett." I shoved him. "You're terrible. You can't use that."

"I can and I will. It's immortalized now."

"And future generations can judge your poor decision."

His grin left me aching. I wanted to trace the curve of his lips. I wanted him to take me back to the office and strip me naked, laying me out on his desk like a feast.

But the lingering fear fluttered in my gut, my fight and flight instinct kicking into overdrive.

"Theo," I burst out, pulling away from him. "Theo should be here too. Since it's his company as well."

I pushed to a stand, brushing the dirt from my jeans, trying for levity as I ruffled his hair, immediately regretting the teasing touch when a zing of awareness raced up my arm.

Fuck.

I cleared my throat. "I'll see you later."

I could feel Linc tracking me as I hurried across the warehouse, his gaze a heavy weight on my back. At the exit I glanced over my shoulder, unsurprised to find him watching me. Our gazes met, held, a moment passing between us that left me shaking and breathless.

Pull it together, Annie.

I deliberately turned away, leaving the warehouse, mentally berating myself for the mess I'd created.

"What am I doing?" I whispered, a tiny kernel of uncertainty beginning to sprout. "This can't happen. It can't. You aren't attracted to him. You just think you are. It's fine. It'll be fine."

I paused, staring up at the autumn sky.

"Please tell me it will be fine?"

The universe didn't answer.

CHAPTER TWENTY-ONE

Annie

FRANKIE'S WEDDING day dawned with clear blue skies, the temperature perfect.

"Hey there, Ms. Bride," I called, sashaying my way into her room, two mugs of steaming coffee in hand. "Who's ready to get married?"

With a startled fumble, Frankie tossed her phone across the room, the cell skittering along the floor.

I paused, narrowing my gaze on the woman in the bed. "You were texting him, weren't you?"

"Only a little." She pinched two fingers together. "Like, maybe this much?"

I rolled my eyes, setting our mugs on the bedside table. "Were you sexting? Should I leave?"

"No." She sighed dreamily, leaning back against her pillows. "He wrote me the most beautiful message detailing his love for me. I was trying to reciprocate and failing miserably."

I dropped a kiss to her sleep-tussled pink hair, taking a seat on the mattress beside her. "Jay Wood is a keeper."

"He really is." She rested her head on my shoulder, both of us quiet. "Do you love him, Annie?"

"Who? Jay?"

She nodded.

"Of course." I ruffled her hair. "Except that he still hasn't told me where he gets his dinosaur statues."

"Theo makes them."

My eyebrows rose. "Does he now? Do you think he'll make me a toilet roll?"

"Maybe for the factory but I doubt your HOA is going to let you keep it in the shared space."

I reached over to snag her coffee mug. "That's enough about me, let's focus on you. The flowers have arrived, the band is on their way, the venue confirmed the arbor is being erected as we speak."

I pulled my cell from my pocket, scanning down the checklist. "Flo and Mai will be arriving with breakfast shortly. After a leisurely brunch, we expect your mother to arrive, along with Jay's female relatives for hair, makeup and—"

"Annie." Frankie laid a hand on my arm. "It's going to be perfect. I know you've worked hard to make this the most beautiful wedding, but none of the trappings matter. There could be a hurricane outside with all of us wearing trash bags, and I'd still be the happiest bride in the world because I'm marrying him."

I poked my tongue out. "You're ruining this for me."

She cackled, giving me a shove. "Such a," she paused.

"What does one call a bridesmaid on a wedding rampage? Not a bridezilla, something else?"

"Freaking awesome?"

She rolled her eyes. "I'm glad to see success has kept you humble."

I heard the door to her house open, Mai and Flo singing here comes the bride as they stomped down the corridor toward us.

"Here. Comes. The. Bride!" They finished with a flourishing yell, tumbling into the bedroom, arms laded with food and wedding shoes.

Mai dumped her donut box on the bed. "We got one of every type of donut in the joint. But two of the bear claw." She opened the lid, pulling one out. "For you, our Queen."

Frankie accepted it with a regal wave. "As you were, peasants."

Ace stopped at the bed, Flo gently placing shoes and a tote bag on the edge. "I brought everyone croissants except Annie." From the tote she pulled a small microwavable container, holding it out for me to take. "Eggs and sourdough."

I made a face. "Bless you for thinking of me."

I'd begun to wean off the prednisolone which had helped to bring my flare under control but resting the gut was an important part of my management of the disease. Which meant, while everyone else got to enjoy pastries and filet mignon, I'd be dining on eggs, white bread, and some lightly grilled chicken, yay.

We ate on Frankie's bed, offering toasts over laughter, hugs and a few happy tears. Hours later—after the makeup artists and hair stylists had worked their magic, and the photographer had captured all the posed and candid photos—I stood at the end of the long aisle, ready to see my best friend be married.

"Ready?" The venue's event coordinator asked, waiting for Frankie's okay.

The old resort sat on the edge of Lovers Lake, which was located in the mountains a short drive outside Capricorn Cove. Once home to a free love hippy commune, the beautiful grounds had been sold to a hotelier who'd turned it into a premium wedding and function destination.

I gave Frankie a final once over, fluffing her veil then nodded. "We're good."

The coordinator pressed a button, music playing gently as Mai and Flo began to walk arm-in-arm down the aisle.

I heard Frankie's breath catch as the lyrics floated down to us. Jay had chosen Kate Bowen's version of Holding out for a Hero for her entrance song.

I glanced over my shoulder. "He did good?"

Tears glinted on her lashes. "It's perfect."

The coordinator nodded at me and I stepped out, walking down to the beautiful arbor where her hero stood in all his wedding glory. I smiled, meeting Jay's gaze, grateful for the love I read in his expression.

I leaned in, pressing a kiss to his cheek.

"Just remember, I know where to hide the bodies."

He chuckled, hugging me tight. "Thank you, Annie."

I stepped back, wiping the small trace of lipstick from his cheek with my thumb then moved into place, turning to watch the bride. Frankie looked like a pink-haired princess, wheeling down the aisle to Jay, her long veil flowing behind her pink wheelchair.

As they pledged their love to each other, my gaze lifted to find Linc watching me. Our gaze held, tears filling my eyes at the emotions I read in their depth.

This could have been us.

I forced steel into my spine, glancing away to dab at my damp eyes.

"You may now kiss the groom."

Laughing, Frankie yanked her groom down, their kiss holding for a beat too long and their enthusiasm a touch too personal for such a public audience.

The celebrant dismissed us, and while Frankie and Jay celebrated, accepting congratulations for their guests I made a silent promise to avoid Linc. On a day like today, surrounded by romanticism and the sweet hope of new love, it would be far too easy to give my heart away.

A hand rested on my lower back, the hairs on my neck prickling as Linc's lips brushed against the shell of my ear.

"You look beautiful."

A wedding guest jostled me from behind, breaking our contact, the photographer calling for the bridal party.

Glancing one final time at the man who unknowingly owned me, I made my escape.

CHAPTER TWENTY-TWO

Linc

"Great wedding," I told Jay, slapping him on the back. "You did alright."

My friend laughed, accepting the beer bottle I'd thrust at him. "Alright? I landed the best woman in the universe. The rest of you suckers are gonna find it hard to compete."

I tapped my bottle against his. "I appreciate that love has made you blind. It means I won't have to kill you if you screw this up."

Jay cocked an eyebrow. "I thought you were my friend."

I shot him a grin over the neck of my beer. "I am. But she's cuter."

He chuckled, looking around the room to find his bride.

"Dance floor." I pointed my bottle at where Frankie and her coven of friends were attempting to do their best

Beyonce impressions. "She may be the best woman in the universe, but her dancing skills are fairly lax."

I winced, watching as Frankie's wildly flailing hands smacked into the woman beside her.

"I won't have you besmirch my bride on this, the day of our wedding." Jay dropped into his best Godfather interpretation. "I'll make you swim with the fishes."

"That's a terrible accent, you should be thoroughly ashamed of yourself."

He shook his head sadly. "What a waste of a suit. I should have chosen a different groomsman."

"Let's be honest. No one else said yes."

He chuckled, placing his beer on the table beside us. "Come on. I wanna dance with my bride."

"I'm good."

Jay walked backward to the dance floor, spreading his arms wide. "You're missing out."

"Am I?"

He chuckled, immediately engulfed by the celebratory wedding guests.

I didn't dance as a general rule. I didn't like the random flailing of body parts, and the scream of lyrics in your face by sweaty, over-stimulated dancers.

Besides, staying on the sidelines had its perks—like the ability to observe the dance floor and one woman in particular.

She's gorgeous.

As maid of honor, Annie had been bustling the entire day ensuring Frankie and Jay had everything they needed for a perfect wedding. I'd watched her discreetly adjust Frankie's dress and train. I'd watched her pin Mai's hair, and straighten Flo's dress. I'd seen her shove water at Frankie, and slip Jay a protein bar. And through it all she'd laughed and cried, and smiled as if it were her own wedding day.

My gut clenched, desire warming my blood as I watched her dance.

Against my leg, my cell buzzed with an incoming call. I slipped it from my pocket, my jaw tightening when I saw Walter's name flash on the screen. He'd been calling with increasing frequency, his rumbling demands intersected with predictions of doom.

He'd been fucking around with his recovery, refusing to complete the physiotherapy and demanding all sorts of medical accommodations that weren't even remotely needed. His doctor had called me to discuss moving him from the nursing home to a specialized care facility—I had no idea how we were going to afford it.

My finger hovered above the screen, acid swirling in my gut, my chest tight.

"Fuck it."

I hit decline and switched the cell to mute, sliding it back in my pocket and turning back to watch the only person who managed to soothe the heaviness—Annie.

"You're staring." Theo plonked into the seat beside me, his face flushed and sweaty.

"You looked like a fool out there."

He grinned. "The best dancers always do."

I snorted, turning back to watch Annie.

"You gonna spend the whole night watching her or get your shit together and ask her to dance?"

I ignored Theo's question, taking another pull from my beer.

"The bartender's been chatting her up all night." He stood, reaching out to flick my temple. "Go claim her before someone else does."

The pop number wrapped up, the dance floor pausing to catch their breath.

Fuck it.

I discarded my beer, heading for Annie as the band shifted gears, John Hiatt's Have a Little Faith in Me playing over the speakers.

I dodged couples as they stepped together, beginning to sway with the music.

I saw Annie step back, making way for Jay to dance with his bride, her expression wistful. I got to her just as she went to step off the dance floor. Seizing my chance, I caught her hand, spinning her into me, halting her escape.

"Linc?"

"Dance with me."

She looked down at our entwined fingers. "Why?"

"Dance with me, Annie. Please."

She wavered, and I wondered if she recognized that this moment had the potential to change everything between us.

"Okay."

She stepped into me, our right hands pressing together, her left settling on my shoulder, mine on the small curve of her back. In unison we moved, our bodies pressing together, our feet in perfect step as I led her around the dance floor.

She glanced up, our gazes locking. No words passed between us, but a million conversations were had as we danced.

I slowly spun her out then drew her back in, her back to my front, unable to resist pressing a whisper-soft kiss to her shoulder before I spun again. She came back into my arms, her head tilted back, eyes wide as she searched my face looking for something.

Come home with me.

I leaned down, pressing my forehead against hers, willing Annie to feel the spark between us.

Let me love you.

Annie

It's nothing. This is nothing. It's a dance. Just a dance.

Only, with Linc holding me so tight, and the impression of his lips still burning on my shoulder, I couldn't shake the feeling this meant more than just a dance between friends. Amid the music, the lyrics, and the romantic atmosphere of the wedding, we'd created our own little bubble.

Unable to hide the emotions his beautiful eyes stirred, I broke our gaze, resting my cheek against his chest.

Linc's hand flexed against mine, his body pressing closer. I closed my eyes, sucking in a breath, desperate to halt the tears from falling.

Why do I want to cry? There's nothing to cry about. Pull yourself together woman!

The song finished but Linc and I remained in place, our hands reluctantly sliding away.

Stop it, Annie. Don't make this out to be more than it is.

"Thanks for the dance," I said, tucking a stray hair behind my ear.

"Annie, I—"

"Shots!" I heard Mai call from the bar. "Let's do shots!"

I jumped on the opportunity to escape, spinning away from the man who held my heart.

"Annie, wait."

I ignored him, desperate to get away from the feelings he'd stirred.

"Annie!"

I motored across the room, putting space between us.

"Annie-bah-nan-ie." Mai held out a shot glass. "Come drink a toast to Frankie and Jay." She leaned in, giving me an exaggerated wink. "It's water since you're not drinking."

"Bless you."

Jay raised his glass clinking it against Frankie's. "I'll always drink to our future."

"To Jay and Frankie!" Mai cried, raising her glass.

My gaze met Linc's, his expression dark and furious.

"To Frankie and Jay," I murmured, staring at my water.

And to staying out of Linc's way.

On a whisper and a prayer, I downed the shot wishing like hell it contained alcohol.

CHAPTER TWENTY-THREE

Linc

"You know." Ren waved his fork in my direction. "For a man who loves cake, you look surprisingly pissed off." He scooped up another mouthful. "Should I be worried?"

After escaping to the bar, Annie had spent the remainder of the night stubbornly avoiding me.

I knew her. I'd watched the same fear spark in her eyes when we'd painted the floor yesterday. She didn't want to admit that what we had mattered.

I watched Annie lean against the bar to chat with the flirty bartender, my foot tapping as my control stretched to the breaking point.

"He's pissed Annie's flirting with the waiter and not him." Theo paused to moan around a mouthful of French cream. "Who made this cake? An angel? A siren? Prue Leith?"

"Who?"

"Presenter on the Great British Bake Off." Theo

licked at his fork. "Damn, I need the recipe. This is ridiculously good."

"It's Mai," Ren muttered, glancing between myself and the bar. "She also made Frankie's dress."

"Your sister is a genius. I'll be sure to heap my praise upon her. Does she accept commissions? Or marriage proposals? I want this cake every month for the rest of my life."

Ren flicked a speck of cream his way. "As if she'd be stupid enough to date a man child like you."

Theo, never one to take offense, raised his arm to lick the dollop clean.

"You're disgusting."

"I'm—"

"Do you think she's into him?" I interrupted, running my hands through my hair.

They both looked at the bar, watching as Annie laughed at something the bartender said.

"Why do you care?"

I glanced at Ren, a tick pulsing in my jaw. "She's drunk."

"Is she? Last I heard she was on steroids. She doesn't drink when she's on them."

My jaw clenched, arms crossing over my chest. I could tell by the stupid grin on Ren's face he enjoyed taunting me.

"Maybe she's just looking for a hook-up. It's not our business." He cocked an eyebrow. "Or is it?"

I watched the bartender hand Annie a small piece of paper, winking before walking down the other end of the bar to help one of the other waiters.

"You should say something to her," I told him. "She needs to be careful."

"Say what exactly? 'Annie, I know you're an attractive, consenting, intelligent, wonderful woman chatting with an equally attractive, consenting, potentially wonderful man but I'm here to tell you to doubt your own judgement and return to the safe shelter of singleton'?" Ren nodded gravely. "Yes. I'll run right over and get this straightened out."

"Fuck it." I shoved up from the table. "I'll do it myself."

Full of wild emotion, I stormed across the room. With a thud, I dropped my arms on the bar beside her, leaning into the wooden countertop.

"Having fun?" I asked, my tone biting.

She jumped, her eyes wide. In her hand lay the bartender's note, the sight of his digits fueling my temper.

Annie cleared her throat, shifting from foot-to-foot. "Absolutely. It's a beautiful wedding. You?"

I stared at her, struggling to control my frustration.

Why the hell were we discussing banalities when all I wanted was to scoop her up and take her home? I wanted her in my bed. I wanted her under me while I memorized the taste of her skin, reacquainting myself with the beauty of her body, continuing to catalogue each moan and whimper.

"We're really doing this?"

Her eyebrows rose. "Doing what?"

I plucked the paper from her hand, tearing it in two.

"Hey! That's mine."

The bartender glanced over, and I glowered, staring him down.

Not this time, buddy.

When the guy looked away, I did what all victorious conquerors do—and claimed my price.

I bent, putting my shoulder to Annie's middle, my arms wrapping around her legs. With a grunt, I tossed her over my shoulder, holding her tight in a fireman's carry.

I'd expected Annie to object but the element of surprise seemed to be on my side, my long stride eating up half the room before she reacted.

"What the fuck are you doing?" Her screech cut through the reception, conversation ceasing as heads of the loitering waitstaff and few remaining guests twisted our way. "This is my best friend's wedding, motherfucker! And you're ruining it!"

Her arms thumped against my back, her legs attempting to kick me. I rested a firm hand on her ass, pleased when her squirming settled.

There it is.

"Frankie, Jay," I nodded at the amused couple. "Best wishes to you both but we're gonna bail." I bounced Annie on my shoulder. "This one is drunk and needs to get home."

"I'm not fucking drunk," she hissed.

"Annie, we'll call you tomorrow," Mai called, lifting her hand in a wave. "Have fun!"

I pushed through the banquet room doors, Annie loudly protesting her treatment.

"This is inhumane. I'm not a child. Put me down!"

"Evening," I said cheerfully with a nod to the staring hotel patrons. "Don't mind us, just a lovers quarrel."

"Lovers? We're not lovers."

"Yet," I corrected, using my foot to press the button of the elevator. The doors slid open, and I stepped inside, waiting until we were moving before setting Annie down.

"What the fuck?" She shoved me away, hands on hips, color high. "What the hell are you doing?"

"You've been avoiding me."

"And being pissed off gives you permission to sling me about like a bag of flour?"

I hit the button to the tenth floor, enjoying her dramatics.

"We need to talk."

She scoffed, tossing her golden hair, her magnificent breasts bouncing with her movement. "If you think I'm going to talk to you after that nonsense you—"

I stepped into her space, crowding her against the elevator wall. She shut up, staring at me with wide eyes.

"I'm going to take you back to my room and lick the cream from your clit." I wrapped one hand around her throat, enjoying the flutter of her pulse under my hand. "Then I'm going to watch you wrap your pretty lips around my cock before I fuck your tight pussy." I leaned in, nipping at her earlobe, relishing her shiver. "Tomorrow we'll have breakfast together and talk out what's between us. But I want tonight."

I let her go, stepping back as the elevator came to a halt, the doors sliding open.

"Your call, Annie."

She blinked, her hands pressed flat against the side of the car.

"I'm not sure I...."

I stuck a hand out, preventing the doors from closing.

"You're not sure?" I prompted.

Her gaze dropped to my biceps, the sleeves of my dress shirt rolled to my elbows. She licked her lips, a spark turning her eyes to liquid gold.

"Just tonight?" she whispered.

"And breakfast tomorrow." I didn't mention my hope that breakfast would turn into every day from now until eternity.

Her head bobbed. "Okay."

"I need the words. Give me your explicit consent."

"Yes. Yes, to everything you said and everything you didn't."

Pleasure and anticipation intertwined at her capitulation.

"Follow me."

CHAPTER TWENTY-FOUR

Linc

Once in my hotel room, I kept my back to Annie, slowly pulled off my tie and wrapping it around one fist.

I heard the door to my room close, Annie's soft footsteps falling as she followed me.

A dark satisfaction unfurled in my gut.

Come closer, Annie. Let me show you what you're missing.

I kept my back to her, interested to find out just how far she'd let me push her.

In silence I began to unbutton my shirt, tugging it off to lay it over a chair. In only dress slacks, I finally moved to face her, gratified to find her flushed.

"Come here."

She moved before my words registered, her flash of surprise telling me she had intended to battle the feelings sparking between us.

I buried one hand in her hair, my other pressing on

the small of her back, guiding her into the shelter of my arms. "Good girl."

Her eyelashes fluttered, her lids sweeping down, her body trembling against mine.

"Kiss me."

Her head lifted, and I relished her wide-eyed look of surprise.

"What?"

"Kiss me."

"But—"

Impatient for a taste of her sweet lips, I fisted her hair, tilting her head to capture her mouth.

She stiffened, rigid and uncompromising, her mouth shut tight against my onslaught.

Not for long.

"Open," I demanded, nipping at her bottom lip. "Give in to me, Annie."

On a whimpered moan she melted, the fabric of her dress a cool caress against my heated skin.

I took my time, licking and sucking, nipping and soothing, relishing every moan and sigh.

Fuck, I need her under me.

I turned around, guiding her back toward the bed, slowly easing her down, our filthy kisses full of hungry, gasping need.

With slow, deliberate movements I ran my hands over the curves of her body, finding the zipper of her dress.

So much about Annie remained the same—her sass, her golden eyes, her romanticism. And yet so much had changed. Gone was the girl and in her place lay a woman full of secrets and dark desires.

"Lincoln...."

Her body had changed, leaving behind the lankiness of youth to grow full and curvy. Stretch marks colored her skin. I slid the dress down her thighs, murmuring my thanks when she lifted up, the material falling away to reveal new dimples and dips dotting her thighs. She no longer held the sweet blush of Eve, but the full-bodied glow of Venus and Aphrodite.

Her hands flexed on my shoulders, attempting to stop me when I pressed kisses to her full belly.

She ran a hand over one of the angry purple marks, tracing the line from belly button to abdomen.

"Striae," she whispered, running her fingers along her skin. "They fade but never quite leave. Scars of battles fought and won against a body determined to do harm to itself."

"From the Crohn's?"

"No, from the steroid use." She took my hand, pressing it against her upper right abdomen. "This is where it lives, lurking and grumbling like a beast ready to flare to life."

I leaned in, peppering the area with soft kisses. "Every part of you is beautiful, Annie. Especially these." My fingers glided across her hips, tracing the spider web of lines. "They speak of resilience and strength. They're evidence of your determination to fight. You called them scars, I call them the mark of a warrior."

Her eyes filled, her throat working as she swallowed.

"You can't say things like that and expect me to be okay when you walk away."

I cupped her face. "Good thing I plan on staying."

Before she could protest, I kissed her.

A near maddening desperation began to grip me, my hands clumsy as I unhooked her bra, tossing it across the room, growling when her bountiful breasts spilled into my hands.

"Annie." I drew one of her nipples into my mouth, tasting the sweet salt of her skin, relishing her panting praise.

With the silk tie still wrapped around my fist, I palmed her other breast, dragging the material back and forth over her sensitive skin.

"Fuck you," she whimpered, her head falling back. "That's good. That's so fucking good."

I sucked, nipped and soothed, loving Annie's reactions.

"Good girl," I praised, hands dropping to hook fingers under her underwear. "Lift up."

Bracing herself against the bed, I easily slid the soaked material from her body, frustrated and turned on to find her pussy bare.

"Who is this for?" I asked, dancing fingers against her bare skin.

"Me." She shifted on the bed, adjusting until she could lean back, her legs spreading wide. "I love the sensitivity. It makes getting myself off easier."

My control shattered, fire blazing through me setting my body alight. I dropped the tie, my hands sliding up her legs to grip her thighs as I leaned in, pausing only to commit this view to memory.

"Linc, you don't have to—oh!"

My tongue swirled, licking at her labia, catching each drop of her desire. Hands trailed up her inner thighs, holding her in place, glorying in the rocking motion of her thighs and hips.

"Good girl," I murmured against her core, sliding one hand up to tease her clit. "You let me take care of you."

Her breathy groan ricocheted straight to my dick, my head dipping to suck her clit.

"Make me come, make me come, make me come," Annie's chanted plea had me doubling down, determined to push her to the very edge.

Her hand snaked down to fist my hair, positioning my mouth.

I chuckled, enjoying her desperation.

I focused, tongue and fingers working in accord to tease her clit, licking and sucking until, in a shower of curses and strangled screams, Annie came.

I watched, growling when her release flooded my face. My cock felt like fucking steel as I waited for her to recover, her expression dazed.

"Wow," she whispered, blinking up at the ceiling. "I do not remember it being like that."

I huffed out a laugh, rising to my feet to begin unbuckling my belt. "I'd be a sore disappointment if I didn't have a few new tricks up my sleeve."

Annie cocked an eyebrow. "Such as?"

I shoved my pants down, my cock bouncing free.

"This?"

She stared at my Prince Albert piercing, her mouth forming a small o.

A filthy moan slipped from between her lips, setting me on fire.

Come play with me, Annie.

CHAPTER TWENTY-FIVE

Annie

I STARED at the piercing decorating his cock, a deep ache pulsing between my legs.

"That's... new."

He ran a lazy hand down his chest, palm gliding along his abdomen to fist his cock. "Ribbed for your pleasure."

I swallowed, wanting desperately to chuckle and throw back some pithy comment. But breathless anticipation danced in my chest, robbing me of words.

He stroked slowly down his length, his thumb playing with the piercing.

"Oh, God," I breathed, pressing my thighs together, ridiculously pleased and embarrassed at the evidence of my desire slicking my inner thighs.

"Uh-uh." Linc's hands fell to my legs, giving my thighs a squeeze. "I want to see you."

Gazes locked, I guided them open, revealing myself to him.

He made a sound low in his throat, one of his hands skimming up my thigh to press against me.

"Linc."

His free hand fisted his cock once more, squeezing his dick tight, a drop of precum daring me to lean forward and taste him.

"Suck me, baby girl."

I shifted, moving to sit on the edge of the bed. I braced my hands on his thighs as he guided his cock to my lips.

"Play with the piercing," he directed, flicking it with his thumb. "If it's uncomfortable for you, or you don't enjoy the feel of it in your mouth, I'll remove it."

"You can do that?"

Linc nodded, brushing his knuckle against my cheek. "This is all about you, Annie. Everything we do is for your pleasure. You're safe here."

My stomach fluttered wildly. "A blow job seems like it's for *your* pleasure."

His lazy smile sent my heart racing. "Suck me, baby girl." He dragged his cock against my lips. "I promise you'll love it."

I brushed his hand away, fisting him tight to bring his thick dick to my mouth. I paused, glancing up, seeing him looking down at me with half-mast eyes.

"Do you remember the first time I did this to you?" I asked, exploring the piercing.

Linc's hands tangled in my hair, his breathing harsh. "How the fuck could I forget? You dropped to your knees in my bedroom, looking like a goddamned queen as you learned what I liked."

I licked my lips, my hand slowly stroking his length. "You started it. You're the one who kissed me, remember?"

His dark chuckle set my nerves tingling.

"Mm, I believe you appreciated my dedication to your sweet body."

I leaned forward, teasing him with light kisses along his length. "Linc?"

"Yeah, baby girl?"

"Fuck my mouth."

I closed my lips around him, groaning when he pulled me onto his cock, his hips sliding forward until he grazed the back of my throat.

"Fuck," he swore. "Fucking missed you."

I reveled in his words, delighting in his show of restraint as he slowly fucked my mouth, allowing me to adjust to the piercing. I withdrew slightly, using my tongue to lick and tease the steel.

"Like that," he praised, one hand slipping to wrap around my throat. "Fuck, baby girl. That feels so fucking good."

I renewed my efforts, learning how to drive him wild.

"Enough." He pulled back, his cock sliding from my mouth with a small pop.

"No," I whimpered, reaching for him. "I was just—"

"Trying to make me come when what I want is to be buried inside you." He flicked the steel. "Don't you want to feel this rubbing deep in you? Don't you wanna know what this feels like stroking your tight pussy?"

Oh, God.

I nodded, incapable of words.

Linc released my throat, leaning down to haul me up the bed.

"Stay here."

He dropped a kiss on my lips, his hand searching the bedside table.

"What are you—oh."

From a drawer, he withdrew a strip of condoms, tearing one of the wrappers free. With nervous anticipation I watched him roll it on.

"Ready?"

I nodded, loving when he covered my body with his, his filthy mouth demanding long, mind-blowing kisses while his hands stroked and caressed, driving me wild with wanting.

"Linc," I panted, nipping at his lips. "Please."

He chuckled darkly, a hand snaking between us to guide his cock along my labia. "You're sure?"

He pressed the sheathed piercing to my clit, rubbing slow circles.

"Yes," I breathed, my head dropping to the bed. "Hurry."

He dragged his cock down to press against my core, working himself into me in one long, slow thrust.

"Fuck, you're tight," Linc swore into my neck, his teeth grazing my skin. "Fuck."

"Thanks," I panted, adjusting to his length. "I do Kegels."

He huffed out an amused groan. "Well, it's working."

I relished the weight of him over me, the feel of his dick stretching me out—but I had to admit to some disappointment that the piercing didn't feel as incredible as I'd expected.

Until he moved.

Linc shifted, picking a rhythm, the adjustment in angle forcing the piercing to glide along my inner walls, the friction near torture.

I cursed him out, sending prayers of mercy to any listening gods as Lincoln drew me into a deep, dark spell that began and ended with him.

He fucked into me again and again, grunting filthy praise as his cock hit my G-spot, pleasure coiling, muscles growing taunt.

"Harder," I begged. "More—"

His hand wrapped around my throat, his body pushing up to a seat.

"Like this?" He adjusted me until my hips rested on his thighs, my head against the mattress, the arch adding a dimension I'd never before explored.

"Lincoln," I whispered, the fingers of his free hand taunting my clit. "I need—"

He thrust deep and hard, his pace brutal. A scream ripped from my throat—I tried to move but his hand held me down. Immobile, he controlled my desire.

At first I rebelled, twisting and turning, Linc never giving me a moment's rest. Then the orgasm hit robbing me of breath—pleasure ripped through my body like fire through a forest, searing everything it touched.

Linc grunted as he came, his pulsing dick driving me higher before I shattered once again.

In a flop of exhausted limbs, I collapsed on the bed, relishing Linc's heavy weight.

An easy silence settled between us, our breathing slowing, skin cooling.

His fingers drew lazy patterns across my skin. His mouth pressed tiny kisses to my shoulder and neck.

"Linc?"

He lifted his head, his face the picture of male satisfaction. "Mm?"

"Please thank past Linc for his sacrifice." I reached down to stroke his dick. "Every minute of pain was worth it."

He laughed, groaning as he rolled onto his back on the mattress. "Your praise is noted and appreciated."

He shoved up from the bed heading to the bathroom to dispose of the condom.

I closed my eyes, exhaustion crashing into me. The stress and worry of the last few weeks eased, the pleasure in my veins relaxing my muscles.

I fought to stay awake, knowing I needed to clean up, and get dressed, and leave Lincoln's room, and, and, and...

Sleep outmaneuvered my desire to leave, embracing me with loving arms. I easily gave in to the sweet bliss of unconsciousness.

CHAPTER TWENTY-SIX

Annie

I BLINKED ONE EYE OPEN, a foul taste in my mouth.

"Oh God," I whimpered, immediately regretting the decision to wake. "What time is it?"

"Early afternoon."

I shot upright, blankets pressed to my naked chest, heart hammering in fright. "Linc?"

He sat at the small desk on the far side of the room, his work space bathed in light. From the look of the papers, half-eaten apple, and empty water glass scattered around his laptop I assumed he'd been there a while.

"Morning sleepyhead, or—more accurately—afternoon." He walked across to press a kiss to my forehead. "Feeling okay?"

The pervasive exhaustion I'd succumbed to last night remained, my limbs heavy, my head foggy.

"Not overly." I scrubbed at my face, grimacing at the mascara smearing my fingers. "I must look a fright."

"You look gorgeous." He kissed my head, wrapping me in a tight hug. "You hungry?"

My stomach rumbled in answer.

"What are you eating at the moment?"

"Eggs, white bread. If they have a banana, that would be wonderful. Greek yogurt or lactose free."

"How about I put the order in while you have a shower?"

The thought of moving my body felt overwhelming.

"Sure," I muttered, wishing I could drop back to sleep. "Just give me a minute."

If I'd been home, I'd have stayed in bed. I'd have spent the day napping and sipping electrolytes, caring for my body as it fought this battle.

This kind of exhaustion wasn't new. Sometimes it would hit me after prolonged periods of stress. Sometimes on good days, sometimes on bad. It crept into my life, dictating movements and energy levels and decisions. I'd learned to make peace with it, focusing on the bare necessities and leaving the rest behind.

"I know it's probably crossed a line, but I thought you might want your things."

Linc rose, crossing the room to pick up a set of folded clothes, my toiletry bag resting on top.

"Bless you." He placed the pile on the bed beside me, watching as I began the monumental task of moving to the bathroom.

"Can I have some water, please?" I unzipped the bag, pulling a small pill box free.

Linc handed me a glass, watching as I began to swallow one pill after another from the Saturday divider.

"Prednisolone," I said, answering his unspoken question. "It's the steroid I'm on to get this flare under control. I'll be weaning off shortly." I fished out three tablets, holding them in my palm. "Azathioprine. It's an immuno-suppressant which helps settle the Crohn's down."

I swallowed them, shaking the final three pills into my hand.

"A probiotic, a calcium supplement, and vitamin D." I swallowed them down then pulled out a small packet, quickly unwrapping the rice crackers to begin nibbling.

"Hungry?"

I nodded. "But they also help with the nausea. Prednisolone can cause stomach upset. I should have eaten before taking it but I'm already late since I slept in."

"Is that an issue?"

I shrugged. "It'll likely keep me up later tonight, but I tend to experience insomnia with it anyway."

Linc grimaced. "That sucks."

"That's life." I glanced at the bathroom, summoning the energy to walk across the room.

Linc held out his hands, wiggling his fingers.

"Let me help."

I glanced up at him, a tightness welling in my chest. "Linc, I'm naked, I'm exhausted and I need to pee but fuck it, we're having this conversation. This is me." I spread my arms, the blankets falling to my waist. "I'm a pill-popping-exhaustion-fighting-boss-ass-babe of a woman. I live with Crohn's disease. I have a potty mouth. I eat hazelnut spread straight from the jar."

"None of that scares me."

I closed my eyes, trying to find the words. "It should.

Living with chronic illness is fucking hard. It's a privilege to say you're well. It's a privilege to be able to roll out of bed every day and not have to think about what you can and can't achieve." Tears burned, threatening to fall. "I leave laundry around the house because sometimes I can't find the energy to pick it up. I started a toilet paper company and I'm one of my own best customers. My body makes weird sounds, and does strange things, and will continue to stretch and change and look like a walking battleground."

I sucked in air, fighting like hell to get out everything in my heart.

"But I love me. I love who I am, and who my disease has shaped me into. I'm resilient as fuck, Lincoln. I've survived my own body trying to kill me—do you have any idea how badass that is?"

He threaded fingers through my hair, holding me still, his dark gaze searching mine. "None of this scares me. A partnership is rarely even, Annie. And by that, I mean it's not fifty-fifty. Sometimes it's twenty-eighty. Sometimes it's ninety-ten. Sometimes you're both operating at a hundred."

He pressed his forehead to mine. "In a relationship you roll with the punches and you support each other through whatever shit comes your way."

"But what," I whispered, voicing my darkest fear. "If you decide I'm too much? What's to stop you from choosing something else—someone else—over me?"

His hands flinched in my hair, a tick starting in his jaw.

"Since you stepped back into my life, you've already

changed it for the better. I hated the responsibility Walter's fuck up forced on me." He dropped one hand to my cheek, his thumb brushing back and forth. "You changed that. Your enthusiasm and drive motivates me to get up in the morning. I don't look at the factory and see a dying business—now I look at it and see the possibilities. I want to be where you are, Annie. If that's crashed out in a hotel room eating eggs, or attempting to climb Mt. Everest, I don't give a fuck as long as I'm with you."

A tear slid down my cheek, Linc's thumb catching the drop.

"Give us a chance. Please."

I closed my eyes, slumping against him. "You're hard to say no to."

"Then don't."

I lay a hand on his chest. "Promise you won't break my heart?"

"I promise I'll try."

His brutally honest answer gave me hope.

"Okay, I'm in. Let's explore this."

I pulled back, forcing myself to stand. "Now let me pee. My bladder is about to burst."

He chuckled, catching my hand to gently draw me back to him for a chaste kiss.

"Thank you for trusting me enough to try."

My heart fluttered, the walls I'd erected beginning to crumble.

"Go order me breakfast." I stood, dragging a bedsheet with me.

"Annie?"

I glanced back to see Linc holding the room phone, his expression warm and amused.

"Maybe don't look in the mirror before having a shower."

I touched my face. "Raccoon eyes?"

"More like boogey monster."

I laughed, flipping him the bird. "And yet you kissed me."

"Always."

I shut the door on him but that one word wormed its way into my chest, settling against my heart.

Always.

CHAPTER TWENTY-SEVEN

Annie

"I'm not sure why I'm nervous." I dropped my lipstick into my makeup drawer, glancing at Mai in the bathroom mirror. "It's not like it's our first date."

Linc had asked me out for a date. A real-life-grown-up-there-may-be-sex-at-the-end-of-the-night date.

I'd never been more terrified.

"No, but you're re-dating him for the first time and that's just as bad." Mai lay fully clothed in my empty bathtub, her feet propped on one end.

"I know him."

"No," she corrected, pointing her toes at me. "You *knew* him. There's a world of growth to be had in ten years."

I sighed, reaching for my eyeliner. "You're right. Can you imagine past Annie agreeing to date Lincoln?"

"Ah, no." Mai leaned back, her straight black hair

falling in a wave over the back of the tub. "You'd have slashed his tires and I'd have helped."

I chuckled, remembering one such night.

"That was your ex, wasn't it? The one who cheated?"

Mai nodded her hand moving as if she were running it through water. "I should have known better than to trust a man named Dom Jr."

I rolled my eyes, finishing with my makeup.

"What do you think?" I pretended to take a selfie.

Mai whistled. "Hey there sexy lady. He's gonna eat his tongue when he sees those perfect cat eyes."

"I certainly hope something gets eaten tonight."

"Oh, snap." Mai held up her hand for a high-five. "I'm here for this level of confidence."

I chuckled, slapping her palm, butterflies fluttering in my gut.

"It should be easy, we already know all the basics."

Mai cackled, her head tipping back as she sank deeper into the tub. "Hell no, that's even worse. At least with a first date there's things to discover. Do you have topics? Should I look some up?" She shifted, pulling her cell from her back pocket. "Siri, find me unique date topics."

I pulled on my dress, laughing as Mai read aloud the results.

"Okay, wait! How about this one?" She cleared her throat. "Do you think eyebrows are considered facial hair?"

"I have legit never thought about it. Are they? Maybe? Oh God. I have eye moustaches!"

Mai cackled, reading out another. "If you could be any reality TV star, who would you be?"

"Oh." I frowned. "Probably one of the investors on Shark Tank. I'd love to support others' dreams."

Mai picked up a bar of soap, pretending to throw it at me. "Boo! That's too practical."

"Who would you be?"

"Marie Kondo. I need her level of organization."

I chuckled, leaning against the bath to finish buckling my shoe. "Are you staying?"

"No, I have to get back to work." She wrinkled her nose. "This new design project is driving me—"

My doorbell rang, both of us stilling.

"He's here," Mai whispered, holding a finger up to her lips. "You can still back out."

"I know." I swallowed, my heart skipping.

Mai sighed, holding out a hand for me to help her up. "It's just a date, Annie."

"With my business partner and ex-boyfriend." I hauled her out of the tub. "I need to workout."

"You do. You should be able to bench press a small car. You're letting the team down."

I sighed, glancing toward the door. "I'm scared."

Mai wrapped me in a tight hug, her hair brushing my chin. "You're grown people with the capacity to live and let live. I joke about cutting off his balls but I know you're more than capable of taking care of yourself." She pulled back a fraction, searching my face. "And, despite everything, I know you still love him."

My heart stuttered.

"I—I don't, that's not—no."

She patted my cheek gently. "You'll figure it out. Now —" she smacked my ass, "—go have fun."

Laughing, my heart racing, I forced myself to slowly walk to where the man of the hour stood, patiently waiting on my porch.

"Oh." I opened the door, pressing a hand to my chest. "Flowers?"

He held out the bouquet. "Actually, they're chocolate."

I took the arrangement, the nervous flutters in my stomach calming to make way for a low hum of awareness. "Are they something to share or all for me?"

Linc's lips quirked. "I may have taste tested one or two."

I chuckled, moving to the kitchen. "Let me put this away and we can go."

"No rush." His voice dropped an octave. "I'm liking the view."

I glanced back, finding his gaze trained on my ass.

"Ew!" Mai called from my room. "At least wait to have sex until I'm out of the house."

Linc chuckled, the smooth sound ridiculously attractive. "Hi, Mai."

"Hey." She poked her head around my hallway. "I'm just here to finish up some work. You going out or staying in?"

He gestured down at his outfit. "And waste this on Netflix? We're headed out."

"You two have fun."

I took the opportunity to observe him, mentally cataloging all the little changes he'd made since we'd left work earlier that afternoon.

He's made an effort.

My stomach began to flutter, my nerve endings tingling pleasantly.

He must have visited the barber on the way home, his messy dark hair and wild beard now tamed and slicked, the hairs looking silky smooth. He'd gone for a smart-casual look with dark trousers, a button up shirt, and navy sports jacket—the effect doing strange things to my insides.

I snatched up my clutch and wrap, striding back to him. "Shall we?"

He caught my hand, halting my movement.

"Wait, let me take you in." He stepped back, his gaze passing over me like a warm caress.

"Like what you see?"

He grinned, stepping into my personal space, laying a hand on my hip.

"You're gorgeous."

His lips were a soft tease, his mouth tasting of mint and chocolate.

"Thank you," he whispered against my lips.

I pulled back slightly. "For?"

His fingers skimmed up my side. "Romancing me."

My heart sighed, a soul deep ache settling in my chest.

"You're welcome." I kissed him again, unable to help myself.

This time he withdrew, keeping one hand on the

small of my back as he guided me to the door. "As much as I want to kiss you all night, let's get you fed."

Over a meal he'd pre-arranged to be flare-friendly, we reconnected, discovering the newness of dating each other.

"I travelled to Australia," I said, nursing my cup of coffee. "Backpacked for three months. I've never seen so many amazing beaches."

"That's a bucket list dream." He flagged down the waiter, asking for the check. "The furthest I've been is Alaska."

"Why Alaska?"

"It was cheap, and Theo wanted to see a polar bear."

I grinned. "I thought you were going to say Santa."

He chuckled. "That too."

"You said cheap?"

Linc shrugged. "Theo needed another round of surgery."

My heart gave a little patter. "You're a good brother."

He snorted dismissively.

We exited the restaurant into the cool air, goose-bumps prickling my skin.

"Oh, it's cool."

He shrugged off his jacket, draping it over my shoulders.

"Thank you."

He caught my hand. "Shall we walk along the marina? The wind isn't too high tonight."

Loathed to end what had quickly turned into the best date of my life, I nodded, allowing him to lead me down to the boardwalk.

In companionable silence we strolled its length, pausing now and then to watch the moon dance on the ocean.

"Do you ever wish it had been different?"

His quiet question caught me off-guard.

"Sometimes." I stopped, crossing my arms behind me to lean against the salt-kissed handrail. "But I wonder if tonight would have been so wonderful if we had married. Would we be so familiar to each other that we no longer paid attention to the little things?" I lifted up, brushing a hand through his hair. "You cut this before our date. Would I have noticed if we were married? That's assuming we'd even still be together."

"I never got over you."

My breath caught.

Lincoln stepped into my space, his hands settling on my hips. Our gazes met, memories of heartache and happiness, and unspoken promises passed between us.

"I want all your tomorrows, Annie. Every moonlight and every sunrise. Happiness is fleeting. I've learned that the hard way." He faltered, dipping his head. "My world ended when I lost you. And now it feels like I have a second chance."

He slid his hands up my sides to bury them in the mass of my hair.

"I'm laying it out, if you asked, I'd marry you tonight. I'm all in."

My vision blurred, a sob catching in my throat.

"But I know that's not who you are now. You need to learn to trust me again. Consider this a pre-marriage proposal, a declaration of my intention. And when you're ready—whether that's tomorrow or in a year or decades from now—I'll be waiting."

I opened my mouth, finding myself at a loss for words.

"I love you," he whispered, brushing a tear from my cheek.

"Kiss me, Lincoln."

His lips closed over mine with heartbreaking tenderness. The familiar hunger simmered under the surface but tinged with soul deep longing.

I wanted to sob. I wanted to rage against the injustice of our separation. I wanted to be the daring Annie who accept his proposal and married him that night.

But my throat remained closed, my words frozen behind a wall of fear.

Lincoln pulled back, wrapping an arm around my shoulders.

"Let me take you home."

In the early hours of the morning, after our bodies had cooled and he'd fallen into a deep sleep, I stared at the ceiling of my bedroom and practiced saying one word.

"Yes."

CHAPTER TWENTY-EIGHT

Linc

"When you said you'd take me on a date," Annie grumbled, dipping her roller into a paint tray. "I expected to wear a cute dress and talk over candlelight." She brushed at her forehead smearing white paint near her temple. "Not get stuck wearing sweats and painting until after midnight."

"It's barely seven." I grinned down at her, the ladder wobbling a little as I stretched to apply paint to the very end of the cornice. "I told you I'd take you out when this is finished."

She grumbled something under her breath.

"What was that?"

"I wanted a date tonight."

"You're sure this doesn't qualify?"

"Hell no. Who paints on a date?"

I pointed my brush at her. "You're the one who said you wanted to impress the new clients."

"I thought you were going to hire painters."

I swallowed a chuckle. "Why hire when you can do it yourself?"

I'd spent the week painting the main entry and hall of the office building. Annie had a week of client pitches lined up, and I wanted her to be proud of Garrett-Harris Paper.

"This feels exploitative," she groaned, rolling the off-white paint along the wall. "And where's your brother? Shouldn't he be here helping us?"

I touched up a paint drip, brushing back and forth to hide the blemish. "This wouldn't be a date if he were here."

"I'm telling you right now, this isn't a date." She stopped painting, propping one hand on her hip, the other holding the roller aloft. "Our dinner at the Bronze Horseman—definitely. Our movie night—yep. The picnic where you ate me for dessert—borderline."

I tensed, remembering how she'd looked under the late Autumn sun, the light dancing across her breasts, leaving no part of her in shadow. My proposal had danced between us, and on that day the fear had retreated for the barest of moments before returning to shutter her light.

Practicing patience had to be the hardest fucking thing I'd ever done.

"Tonight?" Annie continued, unaware of the effect her words had on me. "Definitely not."

Finished with the cornice, I dropped the brush into its tray, jumping from the ladder.

I forced levity I didn't feel into my voice, my mouth watering for a taste of her.

"What constitutes a date?" I held up one hand ticking off the list with my fingers. "Two—or more, depending on your sexual persuasion—people meeting to explore their connection."

"Next time, I'm dating myself."

I ignored her commentary. "Food or drinks—of which I have generously provided both."

"A can of soda, and take out noodles does not a meal make."

"Meaningful conversation."

She lifted one hand, flicking me the bird. "How's that for meaningful?"

"There's one more thing." I set my paint tray and brush on the drop sheet, hiding my grin when she took the bait.

"And what, Oh-Master-of-Dating, would that be?"

"A kiss."

"No." She shook her head. "Absolutely not. You don't deserve any kisses after tonight. You're cut off." She made a locking motion over her mouth. "These lips are closed for business."

"That's fine." I dropped to my knees, reaching for her waistband. "You keep painting, I'll kiss my favorite part of you."

"Linc!" She tried to dance away but I caught her, wrapping one arm around her hips to hold her in place. My free hand fisted the material of her leggings yanking them down her legs.

"Lincoln—"

I closed my mouth over her cotton-clad pussy, tonguing the material. Annie wiggled, her thighs brushing against my chest, the paint roller falling to the ground as her hands settled on my shoulders.

Her legs spread, her pelvis tilting, granting me better access. "You're a terrible influence."

I hooked her underwear to the side, licking her slit. I grinned at the sharp sting of her fingernails as she gripped my shoulders.

I worked her hard, needing her aching and begging for my cock.

Her arousal coated my mouth and fingers, drenching the material of her underwear. Stroking and licking, teasing and fucking, I worshipped my woman, building Annie up to a breaking point.

"Cock," she demanded, hips shifting wildly. "Fuck me. Please. I need you to—"

I surged to my feet, silencing her greedy pleas with my mouth, using her gasp to slip my tongue past her lips, letting her taste herself. She lapped at my mouth, licking the traces from my cheeks, sucking my lips and tongue.

Her hands fumbled at my belt and I caught them, holding ther prisoner as I stepped back, relishing her whimpered protest.

"Underwear off, hands against the wall."

"But—"

"Against the wall, Annie. Now."

She wiggled them down her legs, kicking them free. Her hands fisted the bottom of her t-shirt, beginning to drag it up.

"No," I snapped. "Hands against the wall."

She dropped the shirt, a flush working its way up her neck.

"But—"

I stepped forward, satisfaction and desire flashing in my blood when she whirled, doing as I bid.

I took a second to appreciate the view.

"Spread your legs."

Annie widened her stance, her hands flexing against the wall, paint coating her palms.

I didn't need to see them to know that beneath her shirt, her nipples would be hard and aching for my touch.

I pulled my belt free, beginning to move toward her, purposefully heightening her senses by dragging the leather across the drop sheet.

"Have you been naughty, Annie?" My dick throbbed against the fly of my jeans as I waited for her answer.

We'd begun to explore Annie's desires, discovering what drove her wild.

"No," she whispered in a bald-faced lie. "I've been very good."

I fisted her hair, tugging her head back, grinning at her needy little moan.

"Are you sure?" I grazed teeth along her neck. "Because someone seemed to be denying me their lips."

"It was a joke," she moaned, rocking against my crotch.

I slapped a hand across one ass cheek. "Count."

"One."

I spanked her again, easing away the sting with a gentle caress over her heated skin.

"Two."

I reached a hand around to finger her clit, sucking at her neck. She groaned, arching up, her ass rubbing frantically against my cock.

"Say what you want."

"You," she whispered. "I want you."

"Louder."

"You."

"Scream it."

"Lincoln!" she cried as I pinched her clit. "Linc, Linc, Linc."

She chanted my name, ceding all control as she broke apart, her body bowing with the force of her climax.

I stepped back, shoving my jeans down just far enough to free my cock. I rolled on a condom and moved in, sliding my dick along her slit, collecting her slick heat.

"Who do you want?"

"Lincoln," she groaned.

I teased her entrance. "Who do you want to fuck you?"

"Lincoln."

"Who do you love, Annie?"

Her breath caught, her body stilling.

I wanted to rip the veil of fucking hesitancy away and force her to confront her feelings.

I just hadn't expected to do it with my cock out.

"You," her admission killed me. She twisted her neck, looking over her shoulder, her golden eyes brimming with emotion. "I love you."

I cupped her jaw, capturing her lips in a slow, claiming kiss.

"I love you, Annie."

Tears danced on her lashes. "Can you fuck me before I start crying?"

My neglected dick leapt at her request.

"Remember, baby girl." I smacked her ass, laughing at her startled yelp. "I make the rules."

I guided my cock to her, teasing us both until I couldn't resist any more. In one hard thrust, I fucked into her, my cock burying deep.

Annie cried out, pressing back against me, her body bowing. I worked into her tight little snatch, marking her, claiming her, desperate to make her feel even half of the agony I experienced.

"You're mine," I growled, holding her hips in place, preventing her from moving. "No more running, Annie. Nothing but this."

I fucked into her, gratified by her mewling cries of pleasure.

"Linc. Oh, fuck, Linc."

I worked her, driving us both wild by prolonging our climax, nipping and sucking, fucking and pausing until she shattered, her hot little cunt milking my dick.

I pulled out, fisting my cock, ripping off the condom to come on her ass and back.

Mine.

She staggered, but I caught her, holding her tight.

"Lincoln?"

I brushed a hand through her hair, nuzzling her temple. "Mm?"

"I can't say yes."

I stilled. "Now or ever?"

"Now."

I relaxed. "That's okay.

"Is it?"

I pulled back, grinning down at her. "Fuck yes."

She blinked.

"Because one day you'll let go of this fear and say yes."

"What if I don't?"

I snorted.

"I'm serious. You can't know for sure."

"Trust me." I caught her hair in one hand, holding her in place. "I know."

I kissed her, hungry and demanding, determined to brand myself on her.

I slowly pulled away. "Still think this isn't a date?"

"I'm not saying it is—because it isn't—"

I chuckled.

"But if it was, it'd be the best date ever."

I caught her chin, kissing her slow and deep. She withdrew slightly, our foreheads remained pressed together.

"Can you do me a favor?" she asked, her tone soft.

"Anything."

"Can you immortalize that?" She pointed her paint covered hands at the imprint of her palms on the wall.

I grinned. "Absolutely."

By the time Monday rolled around an arty picture of hands had been placed over the mess—only Annie and I the wiser as to the memory that lay underneath.

CHAPTER TWENTY-NINE

Linc

"Has Walter called you recently?"

I nodded, running through the totals again, triple-checking the final numbers.

"What's he been saying?"

I shrugged. "The usual—hates my guts, I'm gonna pay, the doctors know nothing." I glanced up. "Why?"

Theo shrugged, scratching a hand across his chest. "He's giving me weird vibes."

I snorted, signing on the marked line.

"He gives everyone weird vibes." I handed Theo the monthly statement. "These are good numbers,"

He read it while I signed off on the duplicate copy.

"Wow, these are decent pulls."

I grinned. "I don't want to sound cocky, but things are beginning to look up."

"You're getting good at that."

I met his amused gaze. "At what?"

He reclined in his chair, linking his arms behind his head. "Being the boss. Doing boss things. Sounding like you know what's up—because you do. You're nailing this."

I made a dismissive sound, dropping the statements in my out tray.

"I'm serious." Theo dropped his arms, straightening. "This—" he waved a hand at the office, "—wasn't ever your dream. You loved being a Foreman. And fuck, it definitely wasn't mine."

"How do you know it wasn't my dream?"

He snorted. "All you used to talk about was getting out of this town. You and Annie were like Bonnie and Clyde, ready to do whatever it took to get as far away from here as possible."

He glanced down at his leg, tapping the prosthetic. "Until the accident."

My gut clenched. "We don't have to talk about it. It's in the past."

Theo chuckled, the sound emotionless. "I know you think that but it's not true." He searched my face. "It wasn't your fault."

My shoulders hitched.

"This—" he tapped his leg. "This shouldn't have been your burden to bear."

"I should have picked up when you called."

Theo shrugged. "And Walter shouldn't have been driving drunk. And Eleanor should have been an actual mother to us."

"You're sounding like Annie—woulda, shoulda, coulda."

Theo grinned. "She's a smart lady."

"Yeah."

"I think it's time for you to tell me—what happened between you and her? One minute you were making plans to run off into the sunset together and the next you fucked off to Washington."

I gripped the pen in my hand, wishing like fuck he'd let this drop.

"You pulled out of college, took the first job offered to you. Fuck, I barely saw you for six months and any time I did you looked like your world had ended." He rubbed the back of his neck. "I know you think you moved in to look after me, but really? I moved in to look after you. You scared the fuck out of me."

"Theo—"

He held up a hand, cutting me off.

"Be honest. The medical bills. You paid for them from your college fund, didn't you?"

I closed my eyes. "Yeah."

"Why?"

Secrets hovered in the shadows of the room, waiting to be revealed.

I sighed, closing my eyes. "Mom blackmailed me."

I heard his quick intake, his muttered curse. "With what? Wait. Annie?"

I opened my eyes, slowly shaking my head knowing this confession would fuck him up. "With you."

His face paled. "Explain."

Truth finally saw light as I explained the sordid details of Eleanor's ultimatum.

"Fuck." Theo fisted his hair, his head shaking. "This is fucked up."

I nodded.

"And Annie?"

I shook my head. "I fucked up. Badly. Sure, there were extenuating circumstances, but I've spent the last ten years wallowing instead of doing what I should have done all along."

"And that is?"

"Win her back."

"See, that." Theo slapping a hand on the desk. "That's the Linc I know and love. You were never a shadows guy. This is who you are."

I opened my mouth but Theo cut me off.

"I mean it, Linc. I see you now and all I can think is, fuck I missed this guy. I'd grown so used to seeing you in your half-life, that I assumed you were whole. But watching you with Annie?" He shook his head. "You're a different person."

I grinned. "Maybe the body snatchers swapped me out."

"It's fucking freaky how often you smile. Who are you and what'd you do with my grump of a brother?"

His words landed, burrowing under my skin. "I'm happy. Annie is...."

"I get it." He sobered. "Why didn't you say anything?"

I shrugged. "What value would there have been in telling you?"

"Jesus, you're a dick." Theo shoved to his feet, pacing the length of the room. "What value? How about the fact you're my brother? You could have gotten out of this place. You could have traveled and gone places. When I think of all the times you forked out money to help me—all the bills. You could have—"

"It's done, Theo. My life isn't a shit show. Sure, it's not been all roses and epic adventures, but I'm exactly where I need to be. I wouldn't change it. Especially not now."

He made an exasperated sound, tossing his arms up then did it again. "Why won't you let me have this? Why are you being logical, and reasonable, and A-oh-fucking-kay with this?"

"Unlike you, I've had a decade to come to terms with the fact our mother is a nasty human. Besides," I leaned back in my chair. "I'm the mature one."

He huffed. "Humor isn't appropriate when I'm pissed at you."

He dropped back in his seat, his arms crossing over his chest. "Alright, so you were noble for no fucking reason and it's pissing me off but I'll deal." He dropped his arms, his expression curious. "If you love her, why haven't you married her already? Why'd you wait ten fucking years to reconnect?"

I looked down at my hands. "By the time I got back to the Cove she'd become a shell of herself—her hurt so fucking raw that looking at her killed me." I swallowed. "I thought she'd be happier without me."

"You..." Theo stared at me a beat, his mouth slack. "You fucking idiot! Seriously, you're an absolute-grade-A-certified-lump-of-ground-meat. You could be bankrupt with five hundred cats and no kitty litter and you'd still have killed yourself to make her happy." He threw up his hands. "I can't with you."

"I asked her to marry me."

"Again?"

I nodded.

"And?"

"She's thinking about it."

Theo rolled his eyes heavenward. "This man. Seriously, God. You saddle me with a twin and give me this guy? Fuck."

He half rose, leaning across the desk to slap the side of my head.

"Ow! What's that for?"

He shook his head. "And to think I had such faith in you."

"What?"

He gestured at the office. "You're here. Where is Annie?"

She'd taken the day off, exhausted after a busy two weeks of wooing clients.

"Probably at home. Why?"

"Our home or hers?"

"Ours."

He nodded. "Right, here's the deal. I'm going to make myself scarce. Now, the first step in 'Operation Get Annie to Marry You' is a shit ton of booze."

"She's not drinking."

"For you, not for her."

I grinned, leaning back in my seat as Theo spun an elaborate tale of courtship espionage.

"Why are you still here?" He made shooing motions with his hands. "Go, go. Get outta here."

I stood, collecting my things. "Fine. But you have to finish the monthly invoices."

"I got this."

He pulled me into a hug. "I want you happy, Linc. Don't come back until she says yes."

I clapped him on the back. "Love you."

"Love you too, dickhead." He shoved me away. "Go get your woman."

———

I FOUND her in my backyard spread out on a blanket staring at the sky.

Just seeing her eased the lingering stresses of my day, the tension in my shoulders melting away.

I moved across the yard to stand over her, hands on my hips.

"What are you doing down there, Ms. Harris?"

She squinted at me, raising a hand to shade her eyes. "Watching clouds be born. Shouldn't you be at work?"

"Theo sent me home for good behavior." I glanced at the sky. "Are there really clouds giving birth? I don't see any blood."

She chuckled, sitting up to catch my hand and drag me down to sit beside her.

"Lay back."

I stretched out, reclining on her picnic blanket. She snuggled into my side, her head resting on the crook of my arm.

"See?" She pointed at a clump of swirling clouds. "Watch for the tuffs and whisps. They're the most interesting."

"Tuffs?" I asked, cocking one eyebrow.

"Not a scientific term, obviously. But the—" she made a swirling motion with her hands. "Tuffs."

"And whisps." I echoed, straight-faced.

She shot me a glare. "Are you going to ruin this for me?"

"No." I turned back to stare at the sky. "I'll behave."

She snorted but settled, both of us watching the clouds swirl and dance, tuffs and whisps breaking away to begin forming their own fluffy cluster.

"When was the last time you lay on the ground and watched clouds?" Annie asked, breaking the quiet between us.

"Never."

"Why does that not surprise me?" Her hands lifted, her body stretching. "This is my church. Some people look for peace in buildings. Some in prayer." She gestured at the sky. "I find peace watching clouds grow."

I turned my head to watch her. "Why clouds?"

She shrugged.

"Come on," I cajoled. "Tell me."

"It's silly."

I reached out to catch her hand, entwining our fingers together. "I promise not to laugh. Or judge."

She rolled her eyes. "Oh, you'll judge."

"Maybe a little," I admitted. "But I'll remain open minded."

"I've always thought that if these magnificent fluffy balls of importance can grow with no brain, no intention, no intervention, and still have such a profound impact on the world that we carry apps on our phones dedicated to them—then what could I, a sentient being, accomplish?"

I let out a long, low whistle. "That's fucking deep."

She waved her free hand. "I try."

I twisted back to look at the sky, conscious of the press of her hand in mine. "It's certainly better than what I thought."

"What did you think?"

"That you were looking for phallic-shaped clouds."

She burst out laughing, slapping a playful hand to my chest. "You're the worst."

I rolled, coming over her, lowering until our bodies pressed together. "I know." I leaned in, my mouth a breath from hers. "But you like me."

"Sometimes," she whispered, her gaze searching mine. "Only sometimes."

"Now?" I asked.

Her lips curled up, her golden eyes dancing with amusement. "That depends."

"On?"

"If you're about to kiss me."

I caught her lips intending to keep our embrace light —for my resolution to immediately break when she pulled me down, lifting her shirt to encourage me to worship her breasts.

"Did you come home just to kiss me?" she asked, her cheeks rosy.

I nuzzled her nipple. "Absolutely."

She moved, tugging me up her body. "Come lay with me."

I reluctantly pulled myself away from her glorious tits, stretching out beside her.

She tangled fingers in my hair, her expression searching.

"Linc."

I stilled. "Yeah?"

She glanced away. "Pizza for dinner?"

No fucking way.

"What were you going to say?"

"Nothing."

Frustration boiled in my gut. "No, tell me. What were you going to say?"

"It's not important."

"Jesus, Annie. Don't you know by now that everything you do is important to me?" I sat up, running a hand through my hair. "What do I have to do to prove I love you? I'm here, every single day. I show up. I listen. I'm trying—so fucking hard—and yet you still look at me with fear in your eyes. Why? What am I doing wrong?"

"I don't know."

I pushed up, pacing the yard. "Do you want poems? Songs? Do I need to buy you things? I need to know, Annie. I can't do this alone, I can't—"

"Lincoln." She scrambled to her feet. "Stop."

I shook my head. "You can't give me sunshine every day and then lock it away." I stared into her golden eyes, baring my soul. "No more games, no more dodging around the issue—here it is. I need you. I can't fucking breathe without you."

I stepped into her space, hand fisting her hair. "I'm fighting for you. This is me fighting. This is me declaring myself and laying it out and telling you that I'll do whatever the fuck I need to, to keep you in my life." I searched her face. "Got it?"

She nodded, her eyes wide.

"Good."

Done with my declaration, frustration humming under my skin, I caught her mouth in a rough kiss, not allowing her the space to escape.

CHAPTER THIRTY

Annie

HE WASN'T a grand gesture kind of guy. Linc didn't do big and dramatic. He showed his love in a million different ways.

The painting on the floor. The daily cups of coffee. Gently holding me when I needed reassurance.

I'd thought I needed a big life changing event. It turned out all I needed were eggs delivered to my door by the man I loved.

I laid a hand on his chest, pushing him back a step, needing to tell him all that sat in my heart.

"You're right. I wasn't looking for the little things. I expected big, crazy emotions but what we're building isn't an eruption, it's a tree. With strong branches and deep roots, and we're tending to it, helping it grow a little more each day." I swallowed, tears shimmering on my lashes. "I want you to ask me again."

"Are you sure?"

I nodded.

Lincoln hauled me into his arms. "Marry me, Annie Harris." His lips quirked. "Let's root—deeply."

Laughing, I bounced up, wrapping my legs around his hips, gratified when he caught my ass, holding me tight to him.

"Yes. Now, make love to me with your gorgeous, pierced cock."

I tasted his dark chuckle as his mouth covered mine. Passion exploded between us, hungry and fierce. Greedy moans worked their way up my throat, my hips grinding against his abdomen.

"Fuck." He ripped his mouth away, cursing as he hauled me up to the house, my mouth nipping at his neck, determined to mark him as mine.

"Hurry," I begged, desperate to feel his cock fill me. "I need you."

On his back porch he let me go, sliding me down until he could begin to strip me of my clothes.

"So fucking gorgeous," he murmured, his filthy orders as hot as his commanding touch. "I'm gonna fuck your tight pussy. I'm gonna use my dick to brand you."

"Lincoln."

We tumbled through his house, stumbling and laughing, leaving a trail of clothes in our wake. With a muttered curse, he backed me into the hall wall, dropping to his knees.

"I dream of your taste." He leaned in, hovering for one protracted second, anticipation spiking. "You're gonna cream on my face then lick it clean."

He closed his mouth over my pussy, letting loose a

feral growl.

"Yes," I breathed, eyes closing, hands gripping his shoulder. "Oh God, yes."

Linc's didn't allow me a moment to breathe, his mouth and fingers worshipping my body.

Screaming, crying, sobbing his name—I came, my orgasm delivered by a man completely dedicated to my pleasure.

"My turn."

He gave me no time to recover, scooping me up, my legs wrapping tight around his waist, his thick dick sliding home.

"Oh, God."

His mouth fell to my breasts, laving them with attention, kissing and sucking, his hard cock stretching me as he lazily fucked into me.

With agonizing slowness, we made love. Lincoln's breathing ragged, the sound sending need humming through my body.

"Come in me," I demanded, arching to feel his piercing more clearly against me. "Mark me, Lincoln. Fuck me. Make me yours. Fuck your wife."

His gaze met mine, dark and full of fire, he pick up his pace—thrusting into me, hard and hot, over and over, delivering brutal pleasure.

A scream ripped from my throat, his piercing hitting me just right.

"Fuck," he grunted, thrusting again. "Tight, hot, mine. You're mine, Annie. Say it." He shifted, rebalancing my weight to allow him to wrap one hand around my throat. "Say it."

"I'm yours," I cried, my orgasm ripping through me. "Yours, yours, yours!"

With a curse, he followed, his teeth burying into my shoulder, his dick filling me with hot cum.

I collapsed on his chest, and his arms holding me tight as we breathed through the aftermath.

With a grunt, Linc staggered to the sofa, tipping me out of his arms and onto the cushions, following to cover me with his body.

"Marry me tomorrow."

I laughed, playing with his hair. "Absolutely not."

"Wednesday."

"No."

"Next week."

"No."

"When?"

"March." I stroked fingers across his jaw, loving the rasp of his short beard against my hand. "At the courthouse. We'll invite only a small number of people and I won't wear underwear."

He dropped his head, groaning. "For that I'm going to spank you."

I grinned. "I certainly hope so."

He raised up a little, his gaze searching. "You're sure."

I sighed, wrapping my arms around his neck. "Absolutely."

I peppered little kisses across his lips. "But if you want to try and convince me again...."

Laughing, he dropped his head and got to work, successfully ensuring I'd never doubt my decision to marry this man.

Annie

I stood at the bottom of the courthouse steps in a white dress, a bouquet of roses clutched in one hand. A sense of déjà vu hovered around me like a strange, terrifying cloud.

"You're gorgeous," Frankie sighed, leaning her head against her husband's hip. "It reminds me of our wedding day."

"Does it?" Jay bent to kiss his wife. "Perhaps we should reenact our wedding night later."

"I still have those—"

"TMI!" Mai clapped hands over her ears making a face. "Until Flo and I are getting some on the regular, I'm calling for a moratorium on all sex talk."

"Seconded." Flo gripped Ace's harness, moving to the ramp. "Come on, Annie. Let's get your wedding started."

Our small wedding party followed Flo up the ramp, hooting and hollering, leading the way.

My pulse fluttered, my stomach churning with nerves.

I'd told Linc to wait inside. I needed to prove to myself that more than anything, I loved and trusted this man to have my back.

"You can do this, Annie. He's just inside."

I glanced down at the gorgeous ring on my finger, the light catching the stunning sapphire.

"He loves me."

I hiked up my dress, taking the first step onto the ramp, the weight on my shoulders beginning to lift as I walked to the entrance.

I found the reception area empty, my heart stuttered in panic.

"Where are—"

"You must be Annie." The elderly receptionist stood from her seat behind the wide information desk, pointing to a set of ornate wooden doors down the hall. "Your groom and bridal party are waiting inside."

I flicked her a grateful smile. "Thank you."

"Have a wonderful wedding!"

My footsteps echoed on the parquetry flooring, the warm spring light dancing across my skin as I walked toward the ornate double doors.

I rested a hand on the old wood, taking a deep, joyful breath, determined to let go of any lingering fear and embrace this moment wholeheartedly.

The wood under my hand gave way, my body tipping forward only to be saved from a face plant by a very familiar chest.

Linc's arms hauled me up, dragging me into the courtroom.

"Lincoln?" I laughed, swatting at his arm. "Stop! I'm coming."

"Too slow. We need to get married now!"

Our bridal party laughed, as my husband-to-be scooped me up, carrying me down the aisle.

"Welcome," the judge said, grinning from her spot at the front of the room. "That was one of the more unique entrance I've seen."

I chuckled, stepping back from Linc to smooth my dress, pleased as punch when his gaze dropped, his expression stunned surprise.

"Annie, you look incredible."

"I know. And it has pockets."

He laughed, pulling me back into him, his head bending to brush a chaste kiss across my lips. "Of course it does."

"Yo!" Theo barked. "The kissing comes later, you two."

I glanced over, smiling when I saw him sneakily sharing candy with Mai.

"Shall we begin?" The celebrant asked.

Lincoln's gaze met mine, my joy reflected back.

"I believe," he said quietly. "We already have."

Heart full, eyes leaking joyful tears, I finally became wife to my imperfect husband.

"You may kiss the bride."

Instead of confetti or rice, our friends covered us in tiny streamers of toilet paper Theo had specially designed for our wedding.

Linc ignored them, cupping my jaw, his expression tender.

"Hello, wife."

"Hello, husband."

For our first kiss he captured my mouth and bent me over his arm, dipping us as he fist-pumped the air triumphantly. It would be the picture that hung above our mantel, our joy and laughter so perfectly captured— the first of a lifetime filled with happiness.

EPILOGUE TWO

Linc

One year later

"I'm pissed at you."

I looked up from my emails, my eyebrows raising. "Well, hello to you too, wife."

Annie stood in the doorway, her hand resting on the giant curve of her belly.

I leaned back from the desk. "Why are you pissed at me?"

She waddled into the room, her walk fucking adorable.

"You ate something for lunch that is driving me crazy." She sniffed the air like a bloodhound. "I want some."

I chuckled, spinning my chair and spreading my legs so she could step into the space between them.

"Did you just wake up?" I asked, my hands resting on her baby bump.

"Mm." She covered one of my hands with hers. "Bean is active today."

"And Pea?"

"Sweet Pea is—as always—also active. Our children aren't even born yet and are already terrorizing the neighborhood."

I chuckled, pressing a kiss to her belly. "Don't listen to her. You're perfect just as you are."

"Great." She patted my cheek. "Next time we get pregnant, you can carry them and experience the joys of a foot in your bladder at four in the morning."

I pulled her down to sit on my lap, threading fingers through her long hair. "You're enjoying every minute of it."

She rested her head on my shoulder, her eyes drifting shut. "Not every minute, but most of them."

The twins moved, little bumps jostling my hand.

"Hello to you too," I whispered, rubbing gentle circles across her stomach. "Are you going to give Mommy some rest today?"

A foot hit my hand.

"I'll take that as a no."

"I blame you and Theo—you're terrible influences."

My brother had finally given in to his raging paternal instincts, taking to wearing shirts around the office that declared him as the world's best uncle. He'd become obsessed with knowing everything there was to know about pregnancy, kids, and how to be the best godparent.

He'd even gone so far as to commandeer one of the smaller training rooms and turn it into a nursery. Annie broke into happy tears every time she saw it.

"Speaking of my brother, he called today—guess what he wants for his birthday."

"I don't have to guess, he told me he wants one of the twins but if I want to give him a choice, he'll take Sweet Pea because he's always wanted a little princess to spoil." She rolled her eyes. "I told him where he could shove his wish."

I chuckled. "He needs a girlfriend."

"He needs a distraction. Maybe we should get him a puppy."

"That's actually not a bad idea."

"I do occasionally have them." One of the baby's kicked her stomach, the movement jostling my hand.

"Oh God," she groaned, burying her face in my neck. "How long to go?"

"Less than three weeks." I rubbed a hand over her belly. "Though the doctor said it's unlikely you'll reach full term."

She sighed. "So long."

"And yet so short." I held her a little tighter. "Our alone time is about to be significantly reduced."

"But you're happy right?"

I looked down into her golden eyes, my world held in my arms.

"Blissfully so." I hesitated. "Well, except for Theo. I could take him or leave him."

Annie chuckled, kissing the underside of my jaw. "Liar."

"Dad called."

Annie raised an eyebrow.

"He said he'd like to come visit after the twins are born."

"How do you feel about that?"

I shrugged. "He's been sober for a while now. And the therapy is definitely helping—he's become an almost tolerable human being."

She chuckled, resting her head back on my shoulder. "You're a good man, Lincoln Garrett." She closed her eyes. "You okay if I take a little nap right here?"

"I can't think of anything I'd love more." I nuzzled her temple. "Love you, Annie."

"Shh, I'm sleeping."

I laughed, holding her just a little tighter. She opened one eye, peeking up at me.

"But I love you too. Now let me sleep."

I brushed her hair, combing fingers through her locks as she drifted to sleep.

Watching her rest, knowing the trust and love she placed in me, I took the time to commit this small moment to memory, forever grateful we'd found our second chance.

***

Thanks so much for reading!
If you'd like to know when my next book is arriving, be sure to sign up to my via my website
www.EvieMitchell.com
I do regular giveaways, updates, and promise not to spam you!

LEARN MORE

For those who may like more information about disability, the Australian Network on Disability has an inclusive language guide and excellent resources on their website.

CPSIA information can be obtained
at www.ICGtesting.com
Printed in the USA
LVHW040714020822
724913LV00004B/267